On The Bright Side

JACK KELLY

ISBN-10: 0-9909944-6-5
ISBN-13: 978-0-9909944-6-6

E-Book ISBN-10: 0-9909944-7-3
ISBN-13: 978-0-9909944-7-3

DEDICATION

For the City

ACKNOWLEDGMENTS

Thanks for the Internet, Google Search
and Wikipedia for assists large and small.

Thanks to ADW
who steered the story
closer to coherent.

AUTHOR'S NOTES

New Orleans is the setting and a character in this story.
No effort to accuracy was attempted in measuring
distance, direction, or time.
All faults are intentional and strictly the author's
who thinks he's being clever.

On The Bright Side

Part I: The Bright Side

"It could be worse."

Anonymous/ Ubiquitous

Original Sin

"Jackie Boy," said a voice from above him, calling down and along the barrel of a gun pointed at his head. "If you can hear me, then you must know you've done good and fucked up now."

It was a hard point for Jackie to argue when he currently found himself down on all fours in the street near the heart of the Quarter through his blurred and crossed vision. He's staring at a small pool of his own blood collecting on the pavers looking for the pair of his Chiclets his tongue was telling him no longer resided in his mouth.

A headache slammed against the sides of his skull like NASCAR drivers swapping paint with the one benefit of making it hard to concentrate on the stabbing ache in his ribs, sides, and legs. The fingers of his left hand are currently residing underneath the boot of a second person standing next to the guy holding the gun while offering up their own weak protest at the indignity. Blood rolled lazily down the side of his head stinging like hell when it caught the corner of one eye before pooling into one giant drop hanging in pure focus before joining the other collection of blood dripping from his nose and mouth.

"You're one stupid fuck," continues the voice, "sticking your damn nose in places where it aint wanted, even after you been told to mind your own damn business."

He meant the girl, or at least Jackie thought it's what the man meant. It was hard to tell exactly what this asshole was referring to here as Jackie had gotten himself about knee deep into at least three particular kinds of shit in the past few days. He silently wished this asshole would wind his way towards a more specific reference to help Ol' Jackie clarify what in the hell his point was, even though Ol' Jackie didn't particularly care at the moment. Shut up and get on with it already, just shoot you bastard and try not to make a mess of it.

"Damn son, why don't you just die already? It's all anyone wants from you anyway. I mean on the bright side you'd be doing us all a considerable favor if you would just do so."

The gun hand continues talking Jackie thinks because the asshole loves to hear himself talk. Never mind any thoughts Jackie might have had to disagree, to maybe argue the point, though it was hard to come up with anything which seemed pertinent to the situation here. It's not as if he'd suspected it *wouldn't* come to this. Hell, it would have been a surprise if it hadn't come to this.

Jackie's feeling every bit of the classic blues song about being in the wrong and of being there for the longest time he could recall or cared to. It was a stretch of time into his personal past which might as well be forever for Jackie Boy's inability to recall when it had started. Tonight's activities are just another example but he's been feeling it, if in a mostly retrospective or revisionist history kind of a way, like he's been aiming for this conclusion for a mighty long time and had made it something which had been predetermined.

That bluesman had sure known what he was singing about all right, though the bluesman probably hadn't ever imagined a person like our hero Ol' Jackie Boy here to be fulfilling the song he'd sang so damn well. Probably hadn't expected a living embodiment of such bad luck, such an exemplary run of no luck at all were it not for our intrepid hero Ol' Jackie Boy stressing the point made by the classic song.

Then again, maybe there was something to all this original sin shit he'd been hearing about while growing up though it was hard to tell. It hadn't really stuck to or with him all these years so it's hard to believe it would come into play now except in a sick humorous kind of a way which our hero Jackie Boy was fairly seriously *so not* appreciating.

Our hero here, one Jackie Boy, had a reverse Midas touch thing going on in life after all, so it's not really so terribly shocking to find himself on this predicament here. But this is not where we want to come into this story.

Three Days Back

Was a bright and beautiful kind of day, the kind of day where one wouldn't be surprised to see the fucking blue bird of happiness tweeting away about wishes and endless possibilities for the day. Jackie Boy's not buying into the thought though because it's just too damn hard to make like he can believe it was even possible.

He woke to a fitful day, a fuck he's still alive kind of a day and like each day he woke, he wasn't entirely certain he's pleased to wake for it when he'd gone to sleep wishing for the same thing he did every night: to never wake again. There's no sense in calling it praying when it's nothing of the sort, nowhere near it. Ol' Jackie wasn't calling on any higher source to help him. He'd have been surprised if any would heed him as none had presently as his waking today was evidence enough of such to fulfill his simple little death wish.

Jackie lies in the bed debating about rising as he counts out all the aches and bruises and permanent injuries lying like a long list writ across his whole damn body, leaving him cursing the day as the saying goes. Not this specific day alone though, as much as every damn day and this, another tick on the check list. Just another chapter writ in the never ending struggle between two plain don't like each other antagonists and neither with any intentions of letting up or quitting the action.

At least the rain had stopped for a little while he thought as he tried real hard to avoid focusing on any other thought which might offer a reason to get up and out of bed. Instead he settled on a bad one, like fuck he's awake anyway so nothing to it but to get up.

He rattles out of the bed with his feet slapping against the floor before he organized himself to stand up and manage the shuffle to the kitchen, where he started prepping the morning coffee. He even managed to make it out to the stoop where he walked over to take his neighbors morning paper back into the house to read. Hours pass and sometime in the late afternoon he starts to feel almost human, pardon, ambulatory and itching to get out of the house right into where the trouble starts.

This isn't a story about redemption or about any seeking of forgiveness or even about vengeance or the ever classic of a man with nothing more to lose. The last two reasons given though are the closest to the truth of the matter for whatever it's worth or means. At its best, this is a story about a man, a girl and both on the downside flip of a coin. Two people lost in the grey area which lies along the edges of every society which has ever existed. The area forgotten and often never recorded in any official records or histories despite being filled with people and events and lives lived in their entirety without any possibility of making any mark upon the galactic record of any size.

They both live here by choice and they 'find' each other, though neither feels lost in any sense of the word.

It might be an accident pure and simple. It seems the most likely reason for their paths crossing. It might be something like fate or destiny, though those kinds of big concepts are generally reserved for people in other narratives. Lifespans should not be read or lived like a prison sentence, shackled to a punishment for things unknowingly done.

'Found each other.' may not be the right way to frame the description of what happened but we'll stick with it, because no other phrase comes to mind and there is a need of a place to start with an encounter which is best described as by chance. Pure dumb luck at play really, an unhappy accident, if you feel the need to put a destined spin upon it. Spoiler alert, there are no happy endings to be found here.

People talk about hell like this isn't it, and maybe they're right, but it's a luxury which isn't suited for the dredges of society like our hero Ol' Jackie Boy and the circles he travels in. It's a context kind of thing and a debate better left to smarter people with the time to argue over those kinds of things.

Jackie's feeling philosophical he surmises, because he's way uptown today. Its way out of his usual haunts since he seldom comes out from the Quarter. He's standing out by Audubon Park where the young people are hanging out in the park. He stands along the levee looking out over the river as girls in bikinis and roller blades. Their bodies all tight and smooth and young, all of whom pass him by without a glance, without any notice at all. Jackie turns back to look at the river passing by, one of the few places in the city you can actually see the river from past the levees offering protections from flood. The river eternal, uncaring and passing him by too as he stands there watching the occasional line of barges and bigger ships down from Baton Rouge and farther.

Jackie Boy doesn't begrudge the bikini girls their youth or their bodies with their token tattoos, their lives unmarked otherwise for the most part because they're all just starting in life for all practical purposes. They hadn't trudged enough roads, hadn't put on the miles yet or seen any of the number of things which would cause bitterness to form. Jackie, in a rare flash of anything resembling sympathy, wished out over the river against the bitterness gripping tighter in a reminder of its presence. He shook his head to clear away the foreign thoughts as he stepped back from the river to cross through the park up to Magazine Street to catch the city bus.

It's late afternoon with the day's rain already come and gone, changing the typical little warm of late May into the steam like humidity of mid-summer. Enough steam to raise a sweat on any devil passing through and causing one's clothes sticking to your skin. Another day in paradise, as the saying goes, pone without omens or shivers offered to darken the sun, to serve as warning of any sort, if only recognized in the post mortem often called hindsight and which might as well be called talking out of your ass.

Innocuous is how it starts. Hell, it's how everything starts with him, his signature if singular talent to take a benign situation and turn it into a regular grade A full on shitstorm. This one starts with doing a favor, or what he tells himself it is, and not him having nothing better to do or more likely how he really needed the money. Work a shift or two on the weekends at his buddy's strip club in the Quarter. Beg your pardon, *gentleman's* club.

"Wait, what," is asked at the interruption.

"*Gentleman's* club, Jackie, It's called a *gentleman's* club these days," his friend Booby D informed him as he sat behind his desk thumbing through a stack of twenties which he's presumably counting as opposed to showing them off.

"If it's a *gentleman's* club," Jackie asks him, "than what do you need security for?"

His buddy Bobby D is the man with the favor to ask. He's called Bobby D because he kind of looks like Robert Duvall though maybe a little thinner and maybe mostly just in his face and hairline. Bobby D is dressed like he's walked off of a 70's porno set in a wide collared lime green shirt open farther than it should have been considering his age and physical state. The short opened damn near down to his belly button exposing his hairy chest and providing a visual Jackie didn't really want to have to see. Bobby D's look was capped off with a large gold chain around his neck. His hair was receding and formed a friar tuck hairline cropped close. His whole look was completed with the ubiquitous porno 'stache over his lip. The shirt is tucked into what Jackie assumes are some polyester blend of formerly neon lime pants long since faded into a murky two day old pea soup kind of a color.

The one thing out of place for the look are the granny half glasses in tortoiseshell perched out far down on his beak of a nose complete with the librarian chains. When he's not wearing them they fall to his chest like another gold chain decoration. Jackie Boy decides they fit his persona after all. Bobby D peers over his glasses, straightening up in his chair and stops counting the money. He swivels round in his 1920's office chair. He's looking pissed off at Jackie going on to explain at length how he, Bobby D, didn't know why he bothered at all considering what an ungrateful fuck Jackie Boy was being. Here he was trying to do Jackie a favor no matter how he saw it.

"Pardon me all to hell Jackie," he says to him. "What? Suddenly you got principles or some such shit?"

Jackie shifts uncomfortably in his chair. He doesn't want to risk losing the money or the job. He didn't want to be pissing off one of his oldest friends either when he had gone out of his way for Jackie who reminds himself that he could always try being more appreciative just like Bobby D had said.

"What, you went out and got yourself some morals," Bobby D asks Jackie Boy. "Cause if you did than I missed the moment Jackie."

"Wait what's that Jackie? Thanks for looking out for me Bobby, thanks for the gig and the cash and the place to work and oh what a place. I mean what a pain in the ass place right? What with all of those naked girls everywhere you look and cash money at the end of the night? Yea, fuck, what a son of a bitch I am right? Huh Jackie?"

"Sorry Bobby," Jackie says half-heartedly feeling sheepish despite his decided lack of enthusiasm or inflection to make it a right proper apology leaving it lacking something in its delivery.

Sincerity is the word but neither man knows it or its definition so it would be lost even if ta had appeared in the space between them.

"Yea you are, you fuck," Bobby D says his anger at Jackie clear in his tone as he turns in his chair shaking his head in wonderment saying fuck under his breathe clearly deciding about rescinding his offer to Ol' Jackie Boy.

He allows silence to fall between the two of them, lets Jackie Boy squirm a little bit as Bobby D was more than aware of the man's piss poor financial situation.

"Still a job there for me?" Jackie asks and the long silence continues as Bobby D stays turned away from him drinking god knows what from one of those extra-large go-cups they serve in the two-for-one hour before eight every night all along the fabled Bourbon Street.

"Hey Bobby," Jackie says, "Bobby man, look, said I was sorry," and trails off. It's as close to imploring as Ol' Jackie Boy could get and he didn't like this proximity here. Fortunately, Bobby D knew this too and decided to throw him a life line at last.

"Yea, fuck, Jackie," he says looking out over his glasses as Jackie Boy. "Yea there's still a gig, be there Saturday night and talk to my man Terry, and he'll put you to work."

"Cash right," Jackie says pushing his luck.

"Yea Jackie, cash, right," Bobby D says tired of him and his bullshit. Bobby D already wondering whether this was still a good idea or not and betting heavily against the good idea portion of the event. He wasn't liking the odds one bit and feeling a bit amazed at how this motherfucker could wear out a welcome as fast as Jackie continuously managed to do.

Bobby D's thinking to himself how if it weren't for the stretch of way back in the day, the long period of history which lies between the two of them, he wouldn't feel the need to be doing this at all.

Theirs is a shared history with stints and bits which are never spoken of but always present no matter how many ticks of the present day clock. All of them are debts owed to, if nothing else as considerations, if small ones, such as the one he does Jackie Boy here. Obligated is what it was and unpleasantly so and done without a thank you offered, expected, or asked for. Their interactions always of this nature, occurring in this kind of a way as the both of them were long passed plain courtesies with one another.

They'd walked too many miles together in crimes and wars, through whiskey and women like a blues song or a long hard road of a long forgotten country and western song. Still the hairs on the back of Bobby D's neck were rising up in an alarm which he tried hard to ignore as he turned back to counting money and working his books.

Favors

Bobby D's man Terry is in the back, up the stairs, Jackie's told when he arrives at the strip club *ahem* *gentleman's* club. Up the stairs leads him to an office at the end of a small narrow hall.

The office is so overstuffed it could make a person claustrophobic and make a claustrophobic person straight up insane. Terry is tall and bearded, stretched out along the far side of an old metal desk with a scantily clad girl in his lap and nuzzled up inside the crook of his arm along his side. She's tonight's favorite though possibly not for long and certainly not forever. Jackie Boy cannot tell from here but he suspects it's not love which has her curled inside Terry's arm like that but more likely some form of drug dependency or some other form of invisible leash to tie her to his side.

The small room is so stuffed with endless amounts of crap it's impossible to categorize or recognize anything in the room except for the safe behind Bobby D's man Terry. He has the title of manager which he takes to mean he gets to act like a prick bastard of the first order to all of the employees in a contest to see who he could abuse more the girls or the security.

Terry the manger is dressed in a button up shirt which looks expensive and slacks with real nice shoes at the end of those long legs. It's almost like he's a real business man and not some anonymous lower level manager at the fringes of a criminal enterprise, hiding from the fact this was the best he was likely to achieve in life. He's sitting there at the age of thirty whatever and going on old man before you know it with the promise of still doing the same damn shit X number of years later. Jackie Boy considered it highly unlikely he was going to inherit this place from Bobby D after all.

Terry seems to understand this on some level and it's already turned him into an asshole too. Using is positon to get blowjobs from the girls for coke, holding their jobs over them and not necessarily in this order. His displeasure at the sight of Jackie Boy is palatable and unhidden, no attempt made whatsoever to disguise it.

Jackie Boy's trying hard too. Trying hard to not think of how easy it would be to take this asshole out, to drop him straight past down without a stop. But he'd promised Bobby D he'd behave himself, and it was Bobby D, after all, who he was really working for. The person he was doing a solid favor for and so Jackie Boy worked hard to ignore the asshole Terry.

"You the man to see" Jackie Boy asks trying to be polite, trying to remember the favor being done, and to for once forswear his rule about suffering fools and concentrate on counting the cash for this night's work. Hell, already spending the cash for this night's work. He's counting the seconds in an attempt to arrest the screaming rage at the back of his brain over this stupid fuck.

Terry looks him over, working his jaw like a man accustomed to a toothpick there or in denial about breaking an old cigarette habit of his. Not quite as clear of it as he likes to pretend he is and thinking everyone knows he's faking it and now we're not talking about the cigarette habit here.

"Yeah," he says in a long drawl. A voice which Jackie Boy thinks he recognizes but isn't sure from where. The voice Bobby D's man Terry used as an affectation of something he could never be or carry off. The man Terry trying to go for gravitas Jackie thinks without having the sheer presence to pull it off. Especially not while seated in this shit box office of a *gentleman's* club and otherwise going nowhere.

"Bobby D said you've got some work for me," Jackie says.

"Yeah," Terry says again clearly a man of few words making no further move or hint at exposition leaving Jackie Boy to shuffle in the doorway as he's unable to step foot within the office proper. Even the door barely had room to swing inwards and did so like it was against the idea from the start.

"Quick rules," Terry finally says to him, "nobody fucks with the girls or touches them. Some stupid fuck tries to get on the stage throw his ass out." Jackie Boy guffaws at these simple rules trying to remember once again how this place is a *gentleman's* club and this seems to actually get Terry's attention and not in a positive way.

"Something funny to you," Terry asks him and now Jackie Boy knows why he sounds like he does. He's trying to cop an attitude which is not natural to him so he had to borrow one, playing a dude who exuded both cool and toughness simply by his presence. This man Terry has one slight problem though. He hasn't ever been knee deep in any kind of shit of any kind. This lack of experience leaves the man without any weight behind his pose to carry it off in the face of men who've put some miles on.

Jackie Boy knows from experience looking at this poser how his deepest fear is being found out for the fraud he is behind all the bluster. Sure, he ruled here in this *ahem* *gentleman's* club. Terry probably adored Pacino in the movie *Scarface* and had the poster tacked up on his wall and everything. But this poser wasn't ever really near any trouble of his own or more likely always had someone looking out for him. Then it suddenly it clicked for Jackie Boy, this was Bobby D looking out for this fuck like he's a relation of some sort or another.

"Tell your uncle Terry", Jackie says playing his hunch, "tell Bobby D I said hi now," Jackie Boy says pissing the man Terry off and letting Jacki Boy know that he was hitting the right nerve or the area thereof vicinity if you will bringing a small smile to Jackie's face.

"Man, you the help," Terry says still in full posed tone. "So get to the job asshole which is downstairs you dumb fuck." Jackie Boy starts to leave when there's one more yell at his back.

"And close the damn door when you leave," Terry says. Jackie Boy thinks about ignoring this as he turns to head back downstairs to get started on the job watching as Terry starts nuzzling the girl, whispering sweet lies to her. Pardon, promises, if she'd simply, well you know, do something for him, now just what could it be?

Jackie Boy's not looking back, he doesn't want to see it, doesn't want to know about it, plausible deniability and all. He reaches in to close the damn door, pretending he didn't see her going down to her knees or had heard the distinctive sound of a zipper being worked loose and down.

Jackie's not staring at the girls, he's looking off into a distance only he can perceive. A massive headache thunders in his head from the club's music being played way too loud, music which he hates and hurts him to hear. It's still early in the shift and Jackie's already tired of all the dumbass dudes who are way too overexcited to finally see a naked woman or at least ones whom aren't their wife, their girlfriend or lover.

These guys all engaging in the delusion that all of the girls here are strictly for them and want them oh so much, causing them to desperately act like a kid with his first Playboy magazine or something similar, acting like they haven't seen tits before.

They come up to him like he's their friend. They all have the same stupid ass remarks like what a great job he has here, what with all of these naked girls and how awesome it must be for him and how they bet he never gets tired of seeing this droning in and out. Jackie remembers he's on his best behavior here as it wouldn't due to for him to lose his temper and tell these dumb motherfuckers where they can go with an offer to help if the suggestion wasn't taken to heart and quickly too.

The night passes with few interruptions as his headache grows. The patrons are mostly well behaved and he only has to issue soft warnings or come near to restore the balance of Bobby D's universe. Only one incident really stands out for him when a braided black dancer gets caught in a heated argument with a patron which turns ugly and he has to grab her before she can take the man's face off with her very long nails. Jackie grabs her up around the waist and hustles her to the back letting the other security deal with the patron.

The girl screams back over his shoulder at the patron the entire trip into the back with her shoes and clothes dangling in her hands. She's strong and Jackie Boy isn't entirely certain he'd have been able to move her if she'd not wanted to be moved. Luckily though, it doesn't come to that. The patron yells back ugly things back at her and then at the balance of security as it arrives and promptly removes him from the property.

She thanks him for not manhandling her telling him her name is Eden and he was all right by her. Later this moment will poll well in his favor with the girl Sissy choosing him. She'll tell him how she'd seen what he'd done for Eden finishing with how he'd been cool about it. Telling him how even Eden had said as much, said she appreciated it as not all the security was as invested in the girls in that way. Sometimes the security was worse than the patrons in what they thought they could get away with, with the girls. The girl Eden expressing her slight surprise of Jackie here not behaving as if he expected anything from the girls.

He hasn't met the girl called Sissy yet though and so far as he knows, this is just another typical night at the *gentlemen's* club.

The Girl

The girl is young and small. A petite build with small puffy breasts with very large and pale coral pink areoles as he's soon to discover. She has hard-to-believe-it long and coltish legs and arms which do not seem to match her small frame. Her hair is short, about shoulder length and blondish, though it's really hard to tell in the light in this club. She seems to come from nowhere to land herself in his lap as he sits there trying to wish away the headache from hell still pounding his head. He's leaning towards zombification caused from a serious lack of sleep these past three days and possibly an excess of booze but who's to tell.

He's

The night's almost over as Jack sits in a chair near the front of the strip club watching the last dance of the night, almost done with the security detail done as a favor for his friend Bobby D. He's counting his cash and not expecting much else to happen when the girl lands in his lap. He'd not seen her before throughout the evening and is more than mildly surprised to find her quite literally before him and he's wondering if she has mistaken him for a patron for a moment but it's a notion which she'll dispel in short order.

She doesn't immediately say anything to him as she sits there as if it's the most natural spot for her to occupy, her private place held with a propriety zeal which while unqualified, will also go unquestioned. She has one foot kicking slightly enough to dangle her loose high heel shoe as she sighs and stretches out her arms to settle herself deeper into his lap with a wonderfully distracting wiggle of her ass. Her arms circle up and about his head and her head nestles into the soft spot of his collar bone. He thinks she smells terrific, and can feel how she's soft and warm with a delicious feel against his jaded and undeserving form. Her name, she tells him, is Sissy as she settles deeper into Jackie's lap and sighs quite contentedly seeming satisfied with her current station in life with Jackie of little mind to try and dissuade her when she finally asks him a question.

"What do you think my best feature is?" She asks him next.

He pauses as he takes a minute or two inventory of the outfit her body is decorating or perhaps it's the other way round. She's dressed in a small solid black bra or perhaps a bikini top judging by the shininess of the material. She wears black boy shorts underneath which in turn is hiding a black G-string. She wears the black classic clunky stripper heels strapped to her feet, one loosely. She has thigh high white stockings on with a run at the knee. Her make-up is faded now that it's the end of the night and none of it matters nor does his headache as he finds his attention turned to and intrigued by this coltish delight lying in his lap.

"I'd say your ass, but then I'm partial to that feature," he says being honest as he's caught somewhere between feeling there's nothing to lose and uncertain of what game the girl is playing at here.

"You like my ass?"

"Yes," he replies still unsure what she's leading up to while also being curious about it. For the moment while he waits he's enjoying her smell and the curled up warmth of her against him and through his own clothes.

She sets her hands on either side of the chairs arms and slides herself up and down his lap offering a little grind before once again finding a comfortable spot to stretch out languidly, contentedly in. She sighs as she stretches her arms above her head and behind his neck again.

He wants to reach out and touch her but he dares not make a move, is not sure of what might happen if he should, feeling like they're in the midst of a carefully constructed spell which has many, many critical parts and has not yet been fully made and he doesn't want to wreck it. He takes in a deep breath of her perfume and breathes out over her shoulder, causing her to shudder which is then followed by a momentary rigidness in her small frame. He's afraid he's destroyed the scene until she looks to him and whispers to him.

"You're making me wet and we haven't even done anything yet," she says in a bedroom voice and he's relieved to still be in the game and shocked at how brazen she is.

"Would you like a dance?" She asks him and suddenly he doesn't care to tell her it's unnecessary, he's security after all, instead, all he says is yes.

"300," she replies restoring the off balance nature of the encounter by deliberately confusing the issue further with more mud in the water.

"Not a problem," Jackie replies he doesn't care about any of the details of it, he just doesn't want this encounter to end, doesn't want this opportunity to pass him by like the girls he'd watched out on the river's edge that one day.

She laughs, a delightful little girl laugh before she nuzzles further into his neck telling him how she didn't mean it. How it had just been for show as she gets up and takes up his hand in hers, she seems reluctant to let go of it, afraid to break the connection. He's surprised to find he's wary of the same thing as if this might be a work of fiction of his fevered imagination and how if they were to lose contact with one another it would prove they were strangers all along.

He stands and trails after her as she leads him towards the back and through the black curtains back to where the private rooms are. She selects the one which is the farthest back where she settles him into an oversized chair with arms raised up to his shoulders and still left room for one more.

She sits on the couch to the left only long enough to take off her heels. She rises and turns to the light switch to dim the lights in the room. She moves over to stand before him for a moment, pausing to take off her bra and throw it onto the sofa next to them. She stands another moment longer so he can take her in before she lowers herself to kneeling before him and working his belt and zipper. There's a short sharp gasp of startled air before warmth and wetness pleasantly greet him.

After a short time, a condom is asked for, clear it's not a request, and he nods his understanding. He digs deep into his pocket thinking all the while, smooth ace, real smooth. Luckily she is. He fumbles a bit with the task, his hands suddenly clumsy before acquiring the square and passing it to her. There's the distinctive ripping sound as her more adept hands work the condom out from its package and onto his.

She stands and climbs into the chair and his lap. Her hair falls down into his face and her nose is right against his cheek as she adjusts herself.

"Panties stay on I'm afraid," she says as she places him inside her and settles with a small gasp deeper into his lap.

There's a stillness then before she moves, and oh how the way she moves her hands grip his arms, his hands in turn grip the arms of the chair as she shifts her weight so she can brings her legs up from under her and stretch them out on either side of his chest, her feet placed right under his armpits. Her breath becomes deeper and huskier as she keeps repeating oh baby, oh baby in a whisper like a mantra as she sits up straighter until there's a soft cry out and a shudder.

She leans in to him so close he can feel her breath on his cheek where she lays a small kiss on his cheek and then in a husky soft whisper of a voice tells him to say her name, and then demands he say it. Sissy she demands again unaware, he thinks, of how she's just now crossed her name on his heart, how lost he is to her in one small innocent whisper.

"Sissy," he says back in a whisper to match hers, feeling he's earned something which should still remain a secret, or, more like he'd not really heard her say anything out loud, wondering if he was caught in some slip over into unreality, how somehow this wasn't happening in reality.

"Yes," she replies after a moment of hanging her face in the space between his ear and neck where her breathe gently lingers.

"Yes," she says again as she looks at him through her cascading hair despite how the light in the room had been adjusted by her own hand to a dark which doesn't allow either of them the ability to really see each other. It adds a certain air of mystery so they cannot know for certain about any of the details of the encounter or of this ever really happened as opposed to some manifestation of fever dream or wishful thinking. It's polished with a heavy enough coat of veneer on it for it to shine through though despite the flaws in the memory. That's for later though, right now it's real and right now is all which really matters or ever will.

"Again," he says though he doesn't mean it to be a question. She doesn't respond immediately to him and he feels he's somehow upset her. Feels that now he's broken

the spell they're under and remains still for fear of
breaking it further.

She sighs and sits straight up with a pause but still
in his lap as her arm rises to brush back the hair from her
face before matching the placement of her opposite hand
in front of her and on his stomach. She sits there in the
lone spot of light from the ceiling falling unevenly across
her face. It leaves her face unreadable, unknowable to
him and he realizes he's suppressing his own breath as he
waits for her to decide if they go further or this encounter
is finished.

"Let me catch my breath," she says after what feels
a very long moment. He's well pleased as his hands reach
out and grab her waist first and then her ass as she sucks
in another breath before beginning to move once more.

There's this wonderful look of joy on her face as
she cums, like she's almost surprised herself she has
which Jackie hadn't been able to see the first go round.
He allows himself one pure moment of ego and credits
himself as the reason for the look on her face. She's

staring right at him now, associating the feeling she'd just experienced with him, transmitting something more, something other than instant chemistry turned to lust or sex beyond the pure pleasures of carnality. Some deeper connection or feeling between them, even if it's simply there for the briefest of moments before the connection is lost. He'll never know if it was he alone feeling this or if it was shared as it seemed to be. He strangely finds himself hoping, reaching for the connection even if it's imagined and wondering if she was imagining too or knew something more of the moment.

The spell breaks when she removes herself from him completely. She's suddenly moving about the room to pick up the pieces of her costume as she's hurrying him along. The moment was being cut short now and way too soon to lock it down into permanent memory, permanently skewing the remembrance of it. She leaves Jackie to wonder at his eroded recollection, to pick at the precision of the memory and curse it for its lack of recallable detail.

She'll never talk about the night. It's too much to tell and she always keeps her secrets, as is a woman's prerogative behind the other secrets she tells as lies. This is something for the future though, and not for Jackie Boy to know now.

She hustles him out of the room with her clothes balled up in her hands and her shoes dangling wearing just enough clothes to pass for decency or modesty in a strip *ahem* *gentlemen's* club. She presses a quick kiss into his cheek whispering about wonderfulness before she disappears through a side curtain.

She leaves Jackie standing there dumbfounded until another security guard taps him on the shoulder and says something to him which Jackie doesn't clearly hear but responds to all the same. He helps them lock up the place and then lines up by the bar at the back to receive his cash pay expecting Terry to come down and do it, instead the lead security guy, a guy with a perennial too happy a look on his face is putting cash into each guards hand.

Jackie's in the middle of the line and receives his money without comment, casually checking it to see if it's the right amount. Jackie quickly counts the twenties in his hand satisfied with the amount before heading for the side door and back out into the world with a little gauzy haze still clinging to him from his encounter with the girl.

Stolen Lives

The girl Sissy was someone who could still look at the world and see the wonderment in it. Could take joy in its beauty large and small and who, with a little bit of luck, okay, a large bit of luck would never know or see it for the shithole it was, a backwater rock adrift in the ethers of space and time. But this is a mistaken viewpoint, a skew only our hero entertains in his brain, his unimaginative brain which cannot conjure up any other reality. He cannot for whatever reason entertain the idea she's perhaps more aware of the world than he has ascribed to her in the previous descriptive narrative of her person.

If Jackie Boy had not been so infatuated, so determined to paint it in idyllics, of entertaining the fairy tale, he might have gleaned how Sissy, as she'd insisted on being called, how she knew a little bit more of the world than she cared to let on. She was a little too aware of all of the things going bump in the night, real and mythical. She's *seen* some things man as the descriptive goes before the look away and eyes which stare out past the horizon line and to far away countries which few dare to tread into.

But Jackie Boy couldn't see any of it and didn't want to. He just saw her as a girl and a girl in trouble too, even if she didn't realize it. He felt something pull at him demanding some action on his part, asking him to undertake a rescue whether she needed it or not. Never mind how she'd not asked or how there was seemingly no readily apparent need for any intervention on his or anyone's part whatsoever.

Jackie heads off to the club to work another shift, still working off his favor for Bobby D so he can stop owing his man Bobby D favors. He walks into the club to the back and the stairs, reluctantly taking the climb up to the manager Terry's office. Jackie's reluctant because, while he wants the money, he also wants to not have to deal with people exactly like Terry. Jackie pauses and sighs at the door to the office which, surprisingly, is closed this evening. He raps a quick knock on the door before stepping through without waiting for an answer to the knock made.

If Jackie had known what was waiting for him up at the top of the stairs, what the scene was behind the oddly closed door, a door which he'd only known as closed the one time he himself had closed it after all. Had Jackie any of this information before he ascended, there's serious doubt he would have made the climb and different choices would have been made in the events of the story, and all so much wishful thinking of how things could have unfolded differently but cannot be undone now.

Jackie steps in and sees Terry in his usual spot behind the desk with a girl in his lap which is the common way to find Terry and thus not surprising. Jackie doesn't even really note it until he realizes he recognizes the girl as Sissy, his girl. Terry has his hands on her and Jackie's instantly pissed seeing her there in Terry's office remembering the other girls on their knees and not wanting it for her. Jackie's got an old Hollies tune in his head stuck on the lyric about sitting in a nest of bad men when he decides something instantly. He deciphers the scene as something which was a bad thing for her to be in.

"Leave her alone now," Jackie says, "she doesn't do those things for you Terry so let her out of this. She won't be having anything to do with you."

This surge of anger at seeing the girl in this predicament felt strange to Jackie Boy. He's not sure what it's about exactly, he recognizes its color and shape though and it had been drawn from a deep well which Jackie Boy had thought long capped, a long forgotten pang of jealousy a feeling of possessiveness in all its ugliness. He tries to shake the connotation out of his head and deny it a little too late when he realizes he had it bad for this girl and nothing good could come of it like an omen finally delivered.

Terry's still holding onto the girl by her wrist jostling her as he looks at Jackie dumbfounded his expressions clearly saying what the fuck on multiple levels. They started at how, what and why was Jackie here now and just what in the hell was the idea. The general idea being he didn't appreciate how his business with the girl had been interrupted.

Terry's planned festivity with the girl gone now, he shouts for security to come and deal with the dumb motherfucker in front of him, our hero here, Ol' Jackie Boy. Jackie's stuck for a moment, unable to process how the events are rapidly turning against him when there's a slam of weight against his side and he looks down startled to see the girl Sissy there.

Sissy rescues him by making quick apologies as she escapes Terry's grasp to grab Jackie. She starts pushing him out the door of the office with apologies thrown back over her shoulder to Terry and the approaching security men. It's only later when Jackie realizes her apologies where all for him and his actions.

"Dammit Jackie you can't be doing this action hero shit." she says as she grabs him under his arm and walks him out of the club and into the street pulling him along farther down the street and away from the club and out of immediate sight.

She takes his hand in both of hers and leans all her weight down into the vise tight grip of hers. Surprisingly strong for someone so small but it does the trick of straightening his arm to his side merging her walk and stride with his.

She leads him into a quiet part of the Quarter down past Dumaine and then up and over to a quiet little house on Burgundy. She holds her keys in her hand as she reaches to unlock the door and take him and her inside the cottage. It's an incongruously nice little place which would seem to be outside the price range of a stripper *ahem* *exotic dancer* without supplemental income. Jackie quickly loses the thought as an unpleasant one to possess.

The house is quaint, small and comfortable words that could be transferred to the owner. Jackie's soon to be surprised to find comfort in some unusual calm moments to arrive a bit later.

"Jackie," she says once seated next to him with a heavy sigh, "I'm not in need of any rescue so why are you so insistent about it? Can you tell me that huh?"

Jackie of course doesn't have much in the way of explanation to offer to her so he remains mute on the subject.

"Do you understand me Jackie?" She asks him and he pauses and looks at her trying to read something there and failing.

"Are you sure Sissy," he asks and she nods her head yes.

"Really," She sighs once more and looks away from him.

"Look, if you're going to insist on this hero shit Jackie," she says with her exasperation with him writ clear in her tone. "I suppose it's only right you know my name isn't Sissy, it's my stage name. My real name is Charlie."

"So say it," she says with a smile on her face, in a mimic while she climbs on top of him again in a much different fashion than the other night when she'd just been seeking a brief connection. She preferred any kind she could get and keep for the shortest of whiles.

"Say my name," she says as she moves atop him her lips over hers her hands at his face. "Say it Jackie, say it."

"Charlie," he finally says and she smothers his mouth with hers. She nods her head again with slightly more conviction somehow and a tiny small yes from her mouth followed by a lighting peck on his cheek. She hugs him really hard with more strength than might ordinarily be suspected in someone so small, surprising him with it and her sudden fierceness.

"Stolen lives Jackie," she tells him later in the evening as they lie in bed together. Early morning is starting its ascent outside as the first sounds of the day start rising up.

It's an unexpected and out of context explanation unasked for and Jackie's uncertain of what she's getting at.

"We're living stolen lives Jackie," she says to him a rare blurt of verbiage from her, "not what we deserve," she continues, "just what we have and can take and maybe hopefully hold on to if only for a little while and we're certainly in the last category Jackie."

She doesn't leave any room for anything more to say or be said as she nestles in against his body under his arm with hers tight across his sternum.

He's surprised by her skepticism, surprised to find it in a person who, despite her profession, and despite her current presence in these lower circles of the societal strata, had previously seemed untouched by it, perhaps even immune to it. That doesn't seem right though or an accurate definition, but there was something about , an impression she somehow gave of her being apart from it, just off to its side and partially shielded from all of the cynicism.

"There's no keeping it safe Jackie," she says, "even as a secret but it's our best hope."

His mouth opens as if to offer protest or counter argument but he hasn't the words to explain or express what he's thinking past his own nagging back of the head voice screaming to be heard from the cheap seats about how she's right and he would know it if he could just rub two brain cells together to see what happens for pure for shits and giggles if nothing else.

"So shush," she says executing the classic finger to lips motion which is probably the almost universally recognized sign for quiet.

Joey Bones

He was called Joey Bones. A nickname he'd earned from when he'd been a fighter famous for his delivery of punishing shots. Each jab thrown fueled by a century's old burning rage which Joey Bones could never quite understand let alone identify its origins. Though, if a line were to be drawn and a conclusion reached, it might be said how it was a residual of his ancient warrior culture and Celtic heritage. It didn't matter to Joey as he was a man who didn't believe in any god or devil, heaven or hell

Joey Bones had been called by this name for so long neither he nor anyone else could actually recall what his original surname had been. This suited Joey just fine as we all find the name which best suits us one way or the other. Joey Bones was a street commander for a figure known only as King, who was running a small army of thugs and would be gangsters. King used this army to control a decent portion of the criminal work being done in the city at large and around them.

Joey was a red-headed Irish kid, courtesy of his mother who raised him alone after the old man had been killed or run off or whatever the story being spun at the moment was over his mother's own tumbler full of whiskey. He'd realized from early on how there wasn't much likelihood of escaping his situation unless drastic measures were taken. The typical neighborhood results were crime, cops or firefighting with the army always held out as a last resort option for him. Joey had taken to looking for a way out of where he was from, with nowhere as his mostly likely destination until he'd gone to a local gym without any particular thought to what he'd find there beyond an interest in getting stronger.

Joey Bones had taken to the boxing like it was a calling for a host of reasons. There was an attraction to stepping into the ring for the fight alone until Joey saw the amount of money it offered. Joey paid close attention to all of the money around the ring and soon came to the realization how it was the guys standing outside the ring which were making the real money while avoiding the crush of the actual fighting. Seeing this, Joey became a promoter working up and down the Gulf Coast from Lake Charles to Biloxi and beyond but mostly staying in New Orleans.

This introduced Joey to the underworld which exists in any city but seems to have a special place within its embrace for the fight game. He moved up steadily within this world over the years to enjoy his current 'executive' position within the organization. This was both a more generous and a general description of the loose affiliation he belonged to.

Joey Bones was the man who traveled between the various business interests spread out throughout the city for the man who called himself King. Joey saw to it that the various business interests were running well and meeting the expectations and goals which King had set for them. Joey's job was to sort out any troubles he encountered in the running of the businesses. King called him his liaison between the people running the businesses and King himself and allowed Joey Bones a lot of latitude in how Joey Bones went about fulfilling his duties as King believed in pushing decision making down to the lowest levels of his organization especially with people he trusted.

This also insulated King himself from the day-to-day business, a plausible deniability should any John Law show interest in the businesses. It was a mostly routine job as everyone knew the drill and had long ago settled into the routine from long practice. Joey Bones didn't mind the work and rarely had to resort to any strong arm tactics through the benefits of fear inspired by the reputation he'd earned as a fighter with a fearsome punch.

Tonight's route had Joey Bones moving through the Quarter and checking in at their various entities there, making an evening of it. It had been a mostly smooth evening until he'd gone to one of their strip clubs which Bobby D ran for them through his boy Terry. Terry had his hand in a soft cast when Joey Bones who felt compelled to ask him about it. Terry tells him a tale which he's not happy to hear about an altercation Terry had had with one of the guys working security in the club.

The longer Terry spins the tale, the less pleased by it Joey Bones becomes. He didn't like the story told and neither would King. The interference with the running of the business which was bad enough, but Joey Bones was bothered more that Terry had let this man get the better of him in the very same club he was supposed to be running especially over something as frivolous as a girl. Joey hadn't liked Terry from the start. The man was sleazy without being aware of it and with aims far above the station he was lucky to already hold and without the skills to achieve them.

Joey Bones knew he was going to have to do something about Terry soon enough but first the hero to deal with. Joey's admittedly surprised, at the arrival of the hero as prior no-one was generally plain stupid enough to interfere with the business known to be King's and under Joey Bones' protection. A hero was problematic though and neither he nor King liked heroes as they tended to upset the established order of things for a short period of time. They tended to die in a very loud front page sort of way which in turn brought unasked for attention followed by vows from public officials and the crackdown which followed but never stuck but nevertheless hampered the proper conduction of business and the money which flowed from it.

The actions of these would be heroes were always in a disproportionate ratio of what they did versus what needed to be done to dissuade them from their chosen course of action. If strong discouragement had not worked or the hero was determined to not be dissuaded, than the next step to get them to stop did, of course, include killing and killing most definitely made the news.

Heroes were nothing but a whole bunch of goddamned unnecessary trouble and straight bad for business. Just like this joker here running roughshod bullish and blind causing all kinds of uncalled for interruptions because the damned fool thought he was in love with one of their damned strippers, pardon, 'exotic dancer.' Joey Bones was still having trouble with the fact that this hero would cause all of this chaos over one simple and should have been insignificant girl made no sense whatsoever.

Joey Bones was expected to deal with these kinds of things as a matter of course as part of his job. His only debate concerned telling King about it or not which Joey decides to skip, hoping it won't be necessary. If he has to tell King that he couldn't deal with this one hero, it was akin to admitting failure and was not something he was accustomed to on either half of the statement.

This hero Jackie Boy had made a nuisance of himself in their operations in the city and was a problem which Joey knows has to be dealt with both quickly and as discretely as possible. He wonders if a warning might suffice and decides to contact the two cops King had on their payroll to see if they could sort out this man who wanted to play hero. Have these two find the hero and offer him some friendly advice to mind his own business. It would keep him and King out of it though if they should fail to dissuade the hero, well then Joey Bones would see to the hero himself.

The Dissuaders

Jackie Boy's walking through the Quarter with his mind occupied with thoughts riotously churning over in a small private area of his brain he used to describe as quiet. His preoccupation prevents him from noting the darker shadow tucked in amongst the others. He doesn't see the strike which hits him and knocks him right flat on his ass.

He sits for a long moment on the ground fighting the immense pain seeming to touch every part of his body. Another moment more is spent questioning the betrayal of gravity and the source of the attack as he tries to blink away what seems to be nearly triple vision which his eyes cannot seem to get clear of when he hears a voice pass a greeting to him. Greeting being a generous term for the phrase tossed out with casual hostility attached to it Jackie Boy looks up to see two of NOPD's finest standing above him as if he wasn't already having just the straight shittiest kind of a day to start with.

"We need to talk to you Jackie Boy," one of the pair says to him before they quickly flank him on either side. One cop per arm and reach down to grab up under his armpits and lift him upwards involuntarily. They stand a trio then as they quickly dash him into an alcove out of immediate sight of the street. They throw him against the wall and he sticks there for a moment counting his aches and pains in a posture mimicking standing. He utters a fuck you under his breath but still loud enough for the pair to hear it.

He's rewarded for his outburst with a slam of fists into his lower back right about where his kidneys are located. Jackie Boy grunts with the blows delivered trying to suck some air into his lungs and struggling to do so as he slithers down the wall a bit to crumple back into a heap on the ground once more.

"Damn Jackie Boy," one of the pair of cops says to him, "you should be smarter than that. You know how these things go."

Jackie Boy stays crumpled in his heap on the sidewalk looking up at the two at a loss for words. He has no idea why these two have decided to single him out presently. He briefly wonders if it was some form of retribution from NOPD over his old sins or if it's something of a more recent vintage that he's stepped into this time.

He thinks about the altercation with Terry at the club over the girl suddenly wishing he hadn't had the thought. He's hoping this is for his old sins, a return on some very long memory as he figured these two to be a pair of dirty cops playing both sides against each other and heedless of the damage they cause purposeful or collateral not that these two can make the distinction any longer.

"Jackie Boy," says the other cop, or so Jackie thinks though he's not sure as he cannot really tell the two apart past the distinction of one's being black and the other's being white. From a far lost corner of his brain Jackie Boy thinks of them as the Tweedles for their sameness in appearance. "You need to work harder at minding your own damn business."

"I'll get right on it," Jackie says opting for his default mode of being a smartass which is rewarded with a fist to Jackie's head. A kick is delivered to his ribs causing Jackie to cough out a gasp of breath as he tilts over on his side his arms around his ribs as he tries to get back the breath he'd just lost. The Tweedles stand over him for a moment as they wait for him to right himself before they continue.

Jackie Boy manages to get himself to a seated position his legs out in front of him and his arms still holding his abdomen in. One of the cops he squats down to take a closer look at Jackie by reaching in and grabbing his chin. Jackie shoots him a hard look, or as hard a one as he can manage in his present state. This Tweedle looks up to the other one and says something which Jackie cannot make out or the response to it. He then looks in again at Jackie assessing the damage done while also trying to determine if any of their messages have reached through to Jackie Boy.

"You need to stop sticking your nose into other's people's business there Jackie Boy," the squatting Tweedle says to him, "You following me there Jackie Boy?"

"I don't know what you two assholes are talking about," Jackie says which is rewarded with a quick punch to his jaw followed by another sharp blow on the ridge just above his eye which brings stars with the pain reverberating in his skull. This is followed by a flurry of kicks to his legs and sides until Jackie crumples into a smaller more miserable pile on the sidewalk.

"You feeling me now Jackie Boy," one of the Tweedles says to which Jackie nods his head yes in temporary agreement. He's trying hard not to swallow the thick pool of blood which has collected in his mouth busy counting all of his teeth.

"That's good Jackie," one of the Tweedle's says bringing him back to the conversation he'd rather not be participating in and finally has the good sense to abstain from. He's purposefully ignoring how both sense and absentia are both more than likely temporary things, like an insanity plea.

"So Jackie Boy," Tweedle One continues as the other Tweedle hovers nearby with a fist ready to find Ol' Jackie Boy once again. "You think you can go crawl back to whatever pile of shit you crawled out of and disappear back into it for a decade or two?"

Jackie nods his head in agreement with the offer made by the Tweedles who look at one another and then their watches like they'd timed the event. They look back down at Jackie Boy and utter a pair of sentences which form together into how this was a good choice on his part, better, a smart choice on his part. The Tweedles seemingly satisfied as they collectively relax though they're not quite done with our hero just yet.

"Just one more thing there Jackie Boy," says one of the Tweedle's, Jackie's in no condition to be able to separate the two from each other anymore presently. The second Tweedle leans in very close to him grabbing a handful of the hair on the top of his head which he tugs hard to bring his headache up to the level of a scream. A spray of bloody froth flies from his mouth but thankfully, as a small favor or mercy, misses both Tweedle's who would certainly have made him pay if he'd marked their sharp pressed unis and highly shined shoes.

"Let the girl alone Jackie," is said before a knee lifts to his chin to finish the spewing stream of blood as Jackie Boy's flies for a lonely short moment before crashing into the curb and the street.

A small non-descript van rolls up in the street behind the two Tweedles who rapidly disappear into its darkened interior. There's a banging of doors being slammed shut before the van takes off leaving Jackie Boy lost in the drone of street sounds. The last thing the Tweedle's had said to him is the only clear thing ringing in his head. It is the only item he can pick out at any rate and he wonders just why the Tweedles should care enough about her too have put the emphasis of their focus there before Jackie succumbs to unconsciousness.

Jackie wakes some time later still lying dumped on the streets of the Quarter, which is no fit place to be. He aches everywhere and is rapidly dissuaded from moving off of the spot he occupies when he attempts to rise and the pounding he took reminds him its best to stay down for a moment or more.

Jackie doesn't mind so much as he works to collect his scattered mind. He briefly replays the encounter with the Tweedles, mostly the last part. The emphasis they'd placed there simply by mentioning it, by making a straight point of the girl and telling him to let her go. Jackie Boy not knowing why the Tweedle's would or why anyone else should care about the girl and his relation to her but here they had. It burns within Jackie's subconscious.

It was the one point he wouldn't concede and he wondered what they'd hoped to accomplish by this warning and who was behind it exactly as the likelihood of the Tweedles acting of their own volition was too remote to ever actually be considered a possibility. The pair weren't smart enough for that kind of a thing.

Lulu

Jackie Boy stumbles down bumbling along through the Quarter unsure of time passing or of distance gained. He's certain of both his direction and destination though, like he's a homing pigeon closing in on his destination with uncanny assuredness.

He's heading deeper into the Quarter to see a witch he knew. A woman who fit the classic description nearly to a T, she was tall and buxom with long black hair and of course always dressed in black, long black flowing dresses with a generous cut in décolletage for a wonderful display and if the description has you thinking Morticia Addams. Think of either the Anjelica Huston or Carolyn Jones version in a pick your poison option and you've got the right idea minus the TV campiness of it all and as a highly recommended side note, it's not to be mentioned if one cares for what's best for one's overall health.

She would be only too glad for all his insistent irreverence in the continued use of the epitaph when it stopped. She wasn't holding out hope on it though. His mocking never failed to keep him from coming to her to avail himself of her skills and abilities. There must be something to all of it after all, but it didn't prevent the repetition now old which was also ignored. Some creatures need to be humored and she's already decided this course of action is the safer one offered after all.

He never did touch her despite the amount of time lying in her bed and despite the want to of it on his part. It was an unsaid and inherent understanding as a deal breaker which he understood and respected. Besides, he could ill afford the loss of her or her skills and her willingness to take him in every time he showed up at her door, or had so far to this point. Jackie Boy wondering when he was going to push hid luck too far and thinking this might be the moment.

The Mistress was quite possibly his oldest friend. She was, quite possibly, his only one. 'Friend' was perhaps a tad generous way to describe the situation. Hell, there's a better than decent chance she doesn't describe it as such at all. Presuming, of course, she'd deign to describe it or claim association with him or even the knowledge of him.

He doesn't blame her one bit anyway she chooses to play it as long as she continues to allow him in her door. When you've run as long and wide a shit streak as Ol' Jackie Boy has, you cannot bargain the favors you receive or are granted. You accept the blessings given and keep your damn mouth shut.

They'd met a long time ago, shortly after Jackie Boy's last adventure with the NOPD. He'd gone down to her shop in the Quarter to see if she'd do a reading for him which could maybe tell him what to do despite his disbelief in these kind of voodoo things. This is when he'd started calling her the Mistress because of her resemblance to Elvira as in The Mistress of the Dark. She'd been less than impressed with his pop culture knowledge and hardly amused at the reference and had hated it from the start.

The reading had turned into an unmitigated disaster when she'd tried it. It went from being routine and turned into a most unpleasant encounter for the two of them which barely deserves the description understated. It was like something out of a dark and twisted movie as weird shit had happened around the two in the room when she'd pulled his Tarot as blood had appeared on her hands and Jackie's as well. The next turn of card could best be described as somewhere between horrific and catastrophic. They'd woke up on separate sides of the room with the upended table between them. Jackie bleeding from a gash on his skull and The Mistress knocked cold putting a bigger scare into him than the actual event for The Mistress' well-being.

The Mistress had stirred first, calmly standing up before walking about the room and gingerly picking up every last one of the seventy some cards of the scattered Tarot deck. She'd taken care to ensure she always handled them at their edges so as not to touch the representations on the reverse side. Once she'd gathered them, she'd taken them outside to her patio with Jackie following her and watching as she started a good strong fire before throwing the deck in and staying there until she was certain its entirety had been reduced to ash.

She turned and seemed startled to see Jackie there but still passed him without speaking. She'd never spoken of what she'd seen. Jackie, to his credit, never pushed or prodded on this point with her though he still kept with his insistent and unwelcome tease of calling her Mistress despite her protests against it.

He bangs on her door until it turns to a knock to a rap to a claw and then a relentless scratch as he first leans against the door way, which leads to slouching before it turns to falling to his knees and finally into a last indignant sprawl inside the doorframe and half onto the sidewalk like any other common garden variety drunken Quarter denizen. The door opens and his head drops to the tile beneath her feet with a sharp and unpleasant crack. This time she surprises him by not being surprised at how he has once again found his way to her door, broken once more. She sighs and mutters more to herself than actually speaking to him a single simple question which should be the title of his autobiography or on his tombstone as if there's a difference.

"You look like hell," he hears her say despite how it's hard for words to penetrate past the denseness enveloping his head, swallowing it like he's underwater or something similar.

"You should see the other guy, not a mark on him," Jackie says to her repeating an old, old joke like he's trying to prove his incoherency. From somewhere deep in his brain he knows the word for him presently is shock. He's in shock and shock is a killer which could prove more fatal than the gunshot causing all this damned hard ringing about the insides of his skull. Fortune had smiled on Ol' Jackie Boy though once more in her never ending bounty showered over him and has seen his stupid ass.

"Right smartass," she said in a tone of voice which was as dry as the desert. The tone complimented her body language which could hardly be described as welcome to see him let alone inviting, "What now?"

"Could use a cure for what ails me," Jackie Boy says like it isn't obvious to see already.

"No doubt," The Mistress says after a long pause in which Ol' Jackie Boy can almost physically feel her as she's looking him up and down. Mostly down before she opens the door while still standing behind it allowing him to pass into her house and into the front living room by the slimmest of margins.

"What am I going to do with you," her question said aloud as Jackie Boy heads to her couch which is his usual haunt when he comes a calling. Glad to do it as he knows he has only a moment more of standing before he falls down. She walks away for a moment to disappear into her house so completely that Jackie couldn't even hear her anymore. It was an ability of hers which he'd never gotten used to as her home was a fairly small space with every nook and cranny stuffed leaving nowhere to

disappear or hide anywhere which left Jackie wondering
how she managed it.

The quiet with which she moved about her house
caused Jackie to have to suppress the urge to string a bell
on her somewhere. He instinctively knew though how
that would fairly seriously not be tolerated and he felt the
limits of his ability to push her general kindness didn't
stretch that far or wide.

"Jackie," she says from somewhere behind him as
he sat on her couch in her living room. Her voice is
always tinged with a low almost honeyed sweetness to it
but there's also a touch of annoyance or exasperation in it
as well. He supposes this undertone is mostly his fault for
always putting upon her and about to do so once again.

She never asks him the how or why of his arriving
at her door once more. She just begins to examine him
for injuries and tending to them without questions. She
hasn't yet been stymied by any injury he's brought or his
general appearance and condition when he arrives at her
door. She hasn't yet turned him away either and he's

grateful for the random acts of kindness and care on her part, damn near eternally so.

"What have you gone and got yourself into now Jackie," she asks him while she's pressing a cool cloth to his forehead and rummages through her kit for an ace wrap. Jackie tells her a little part of the story of his encounter with the Tweedles as he gives himself over to her ministrations. The Mistress listens silently, merely shaking her head in disbelief at Jackie's ability to get in these situations.

"Playing hero again are we Jackie," she asks him and he shoots her a glance which confirms what she'd suspected from the start. Jackie can offer little in the way of protestation of her assessment though. He has no defense and is still in need of her medical attentions to risk it anyway and decides to say nothing about it.

"You know this hero shit isn't for you Jackie," The Mistress says as she finished up with her attentions.

"This hero shit doesn't suit you Jackie and if you keep at it you're going to get yourself killed," she says as she finishes what she can do for him presently.

"Well then," Jackie carelessly says to her, "won't you feel just awful if I get myself dead tomorrow?"

The Mistress' whole body freezes in place almost instantly as she stops everything she'd been doing. "Not funny Jackie," she says literally throwing the towel at him and disappears into her house leaving Jackie sitting there on her couch in his shorts and bandages dumbfounded with the out loud mistake he'd made.

Jackie Boy's wishing for a bottle of whiskey to crawl into to get away from the regret he was feeling. He sits on her couch feeling awkward and not sure if he's supposed to stay or go which is soon solved when he succumbs to the pull of sleep.

Jackie Boy wakes the next morning to the complaints of multiple aches and pains which shoot through his body if reduced to a dull throb. He counts his teeth with his tongue until he's satisfied they're mostly still there. He still has a headache pounding around his skull like an eight hundred pound gorilla in a small room but doesn't think it's likely to depart any time soon. Jackie Boy notes that The Mistress isn't awake yet which gives him the opportunity to skulk out of her house before he has to face her and the last stupid thing he'd said to her the night before.

Sissy

Jackie Boy makes his way out away from the Mistress' house stumbling along the early morning streets of the Quarter like many a drunk can be seen in this city. He's mostly directionless as he moves through the Quarter roughly heading towards Canal. He stumbles on the uneven sidewalk and into the street when he tries to correct his fall he catches his toe on the curb and stumbles headlong to the street.

He's still there a minute later except when he looks up he sees the girl looking down at him causing Jackie to have to blink his eyes uncertain at what he's seeing. Her coat is buttoned up to her throat and her hands in her pockets. Her face is washed and scrubbed free from her working colors. Her hair pulled back from her face and tucked tightly into a bun on the back of her head with a black hairband. He can see she's still wearing her white stockings on her legs which are tapering into a pair of well-worn and scuffed Converse All-Stars, red with a white toe. He thinks to himself how she's looking cute as hell as he looks up her legs to take in the whole of her.

"Fancy meeting you here," she says still looking down at him. She's always seemingly above him in some shape, fashion or form. "You know all the best places!"

"I was just on my way to see you," Jackie tells her.

"Aint you sweet," she replies her hands stuffed into the pockets of her jacket. Silence follows as she looks around her and then back at him like she's engaged in some quiet debate which ends when she sighs and he swears he can see her breath even if it's the wrong season for it.

"You look a little fucked up," she says to him letting him know it was going to be alright.

"I've felt better for sure,' Jackie replies as another sigh leaves her. She seems to fight for a moment what she knows she's going to do anyway and regrets be damned or rued later more likely. She already knows in advance though how it's of no help whatsoever.

"C'mon," she says decision made as she takes her hands from her pockets and bunny dips down to extend her hands out to him. "Can't stay there all night," she says, "so let's go," and she gestures the universal c'mere with her hand.

He rises up enough to reach and puts his stained hand in hers as she literally picks his stupid ass up and out of the street. He tries hard not to lean on her or touch her because he doesn't want to imbue any of her whites with god knows what he's rolled in after a fall into the streets of the Quarter.

She takes him back to her place and throws him in the shower clothes and all where he stays with his head hanging underneath the stream of too hot water letting it work its way down. He's interrupted by small hands at his

shirts buttons working them undone and then to his
pants to unbuckle them. The black khakis are pulled
down and he steps out of them as they are thrown out to
the tiled floor with his shirt to follow. She's stepped out
of her own clothes and now stands naked except for a
layer of soap in front of him as she showers with him.
She presses her body against his and uses it to soap him
down with her breasts which he finds is both arousing
and soothing til she turns him around and does the same
to his back. He damn near cums as she reaches around to
scrub between his legs.

The two are sitting on her couch where she's
wrapped around him as she applies mercurochrome to his
cuts. He's mostly ignoring the stings, or trying to minus
the occasional flinch which causes her to literally furrow
her brow at him scolding him for being such a pussy. It's
strange for him to be receiving this care from her on her
couch as opposed to the usual care of the Mistress and
her couch.

After the first aid has been completed or at least to
the end of her abilities and probably both of their

patience levels, she sits off to his side with her legs stretched across his lap with a faraway look in her expression. Jackie doesn't know it yet but will soon how she's been doing some deep thinking on the ways of the world and has a concern needing to be voiced.

"Let's get some things straight here Jackie," she says with her attention unwavering from her appointed task, "you're no white knight and I'm not a damsel in distress, so you really need to stop this hero shit Jackie. It doesn't suit you."

"There's nothing to be done about anything anyway," she says right when he'd thought she's finished but she'd only been pausing. He looks away from her. She has a flash of temper which boils her a soft pink and she jerks his head back so he's facing her.

"Hey! You listening to me Jackie? Am I getting through to you?" She asks. She can't possibly know of course but our boy, our hero, had already heard this phrase once before tonight even as she knocks on his skull; "hello," she says, "you reading me?"

But no reply comes back to her. Exasperated, she leans back and the towel she's wearing falls down between them revealing her small breasts still a little wet from the shower and marked red from the coarseness of the towel. Her hair is slicked back and still damp, her face bare, if crinkled with a bit of anger.

"What's to be done with you," she asks aloud her tone sad with the saying he thinks or maybe tired. The question floats unanswered as it was meant to. It had been directed to no one in particular and he certainly hopes not to him. It's the one question he's never had an answer to anyway.

There are no answers to offer, no bargain to make, and no compromise to be reached. He's already decided to ignore her advice and help her anyway, he'll just have to go about it a little differently and apply a little nuance, some subtlety while pretending the he knows how to. He lies to her first with a nod of his head, then again as he tells her out loud he understands. Jackie will accede to her wishes but he cannot bring himself to raise his eyes to her. It's a clear cut sign of evasiveness, of lying and they both know it and they both choose to believe it anyway.

She kisses him hard and for a moment he's sick knowing what he does and wishing he could read her thoughts though, luckily, it's fleeting. He doesn't think he'd be real pleased to have access to her thoughts right now and he damn well knows it would not be reciprocated. He tosses all this aside because she's kissing him and he doesn't need to know more when she's kissing him, when she's soon give herself again to him or is it takes from him. He doesn't know nor care. She's giving to him he thinks, and each time she does it's akin to some form of gift or something. Manna from heaven, something to be treasured or prized certainly and not to be ignored and he loses himself in her.

"This isn't fate Jackie," she says to him after a long silence, "its happenstance and no matter how hard we try otherwise we can never change the fact we didn't mean to be here now. There were a thousand different destinations in mind and this is an accident. There's no other word for it Jackie."

This is where Jackie inconveniently and unpleasantly remembers, while trying to suppress it, how he should not be charged with skittish or fragile things. He doesn't have the touch for it. Things not for him as Bobby D would tell him. He's trying hard to stay focused on what she's saying to him because it seems to be oh so very important. She seems so serious and earnest as she tries to explain to him the way things are for the two of them. He's hoping like all hell this is some random thought of hers as opposed to some awful and completely transparent foreshadowing device as he grabs up the girl to him in a giant bear hug grip.

"I've got you baby girl," he says and hopes like all hell it's not a lie he's telling on either one of them as she kisses him. The kiss is just a peck at first but quickly becomes something else with a tinge of hunger or need though both are descriptors which they preferred versus the one word they can both taste in each other's mouth but neither want to confess or admit to of desperation there. Neither knows why this feeling would rise up in themselves as individuals or as a together act or as together an act as their couplings could ever be described.

Hunger drives them closer, deeper into one another turning things more primal making the sex hotter and harder. Bruises will be left on skin where fingers and teeth have sunk in when they take each other in an act which is more akin to forms of combat than loving in its levels of violence and non-compromise. No quarter asked or given, no peace to be made and despite all of this there is a certain quality of sanctuary they're able to find in one another's arms. A safe harbor from the rest of the world until they should part and exit these walls for the blinding light of the new sun which they'd been able to ignore so long as they'd stayed where they'd been but is not to be.

The day calls them back to reality which is cold clear and hard in the yellow grim rays of the sun to be trudged through until the night turns back around to fall upon and hide all of the unpleasantries which shrink from the touch of the sun. The girl's still in a state of half sleep or other form of near consciousness with her back pressed to him and her hands tucked under her head like a child or perhaps an innocents for a better use of word here when she says something to him, and he just knows it's going to knock around and haunt him for a very long time.

"This city is your woman Jackie," she says softly, wistfully and with a touch of resignation or sadness, "she's exotic and exciting and nothing and nobody else comes close to comparison with her or can and it's unfair of you Jackie to pretend otherwise."

Jackie Boy lays on his back the sweat on his body suddenly feeling cold with a restlessness stirring deep in his bones. He's bothered more than he cares to admit about what the girl has said in her sleep despite knowing that things said in the dark cannot be held against a person comes the morning light. What he should do is shift his weight and put his arm on her shoulder, turn her back to him and kiss her hard. Desperate to steal the truth from her lips and make her unbelieve the words she'd just spoken, to erase any doubt lingering there when he makes love to her.

Were he capable of these kinds of things he just might have. He isn't and instead he lays there in the dark

looking at her naked back. There's light on her shoulder
and her blonde hair splayed on the pillow as the rain
begins a steady tapping on the roof and windows of their
now silent room.

pages from the girl's diary

Charlie's thinking about her attraction to Jackie Boy
wondering where in the hell it had come from, at the gall
of its appearance. The shear gall of it to spring forth like
this and cause her to return to the impulsiveness she'd
worked so hard to get herself past. Creeping up on her to
spring unannounced and unwelcome too. Something pure
crazy she thinks because it's gotta be something which's
causing her to act this way.

She'd long ago given up on any notion of love as
she knew it too well for the fiction it was to ever give it
any lee way or space within her life and then this
damnded bad penny which keeps turning up. An apt
description for finding him in the street like she had.
Clearly they had some kind of a connection whether she

wanted it or not, whether she believed it or not, there it was all the same. She sighs a very long sigh from deep down and out from her diaphragm leaving her to shaking her head because she cannot get over this Jackie Boy character, cannot make heads or tails of any part of it.

She hadn't been kidding when she'd told him it wasn't fate which had brought them into each other's lives. She knew it was accident more than any other thing though she couldn't particularly explain how they kept running into each other at random intervals. It defied explanation even in a city as small as New Orleans is and was too damn spooky.

Strangely, she felt it was unfair too. Unfair how it should come rolling along and intrusive when she'd finally felt like she'd gotten something's settled and into a comfortable array. Comfortable enough for her to live with them at any rate and then this man called Jackie Boy had kept popping up out of nowhere and unsettling things. She sighs, a long sigh too, as she didn't know what was to be done about any of it, assuming there was a possibility to be arrived at.

This guy's not to be believed she thinks to herself, keeps telling herself as she recounts the charge she'd felt through her body when his breathe had passed over her shoulder back at the club in their first meeting. She'd responded to the sudden rush of connection or weird chemistry she'd felt in the moment and now was kicking herself over it. It was fine for her to give into a rash moment there, but not for the lingering in her head like the guy's currently occupying in her brain.

Something about him and her though despite how it didn't make any kind of a sense at all. Attraction follows no laws, rules or lines of thought as she well knew, charting its own path and connecting people who most probably otherwise had no business with one another. She and he were connected somehow, someway is really the only explanation because otherwise it doesn't make sense or she doesn't want it to. It's why they kept falling in and out of each other's lives like they do. Some others might call this fate, hell some might even give into it and call it love like it's some kind of sweet thing when she well knows it's not.

She knows how it's a sickness, a disease like a plague, and one which she's been trying to avoid for quite some time now. Sickness is the only way to describe it as she was left without any other way to explain what had drawn her to him when she'd seen him at the club and then went and sat in his lap. She wants to blame it on compulsiveness which she was known to experience from time to time but cannot. This feels like it was somehow, someway, something more and she shouldn't get more specific which was really annoying her. The pestering notion of trying to explain the why of her out of character behavior this evening proving itself unintentionally clingy to her person.

This Jackie Boy character with a penchant towards doing god damned hero shit, she just knew it, could read it in his character like it had been writ in his skin. She couldn't shake him off it either despite her repeated implorations leaving her wishing she'd just stayed away from him from the start.

And this is where the trouble starts.

Part II: Good Intentions

The road to hell is paved with good intentions.

- Saint Bernard of Clairvaux

Where Trouble Starts

Jackie Boy spends the next morning deciding he was going to put things straight because he's unable to leave well enough alone. He decides he'll go down to the club to see Terry and explain to him that neither he nor the girl is going to be working at the club anymore. He knows Terry won't be sorry to see him go and wonders if Terry will feel the same about the girl.

Jackie enters the club going straight to the back stairs to make the climb up to Terry's office. He doesn't knock as he enters the cramped room and is mildly surprised to see Terry in there all by his lonesome for a change. Terry's caught off guard by the unexpected arrival of Jackie Boy and tells him flat out how he'd never thought he'd see him again while silently wondering what the hell had happened to the security downstairs which had allowed this fucker to walk right into the club and then up to Terry's office. Somebody was going to be getting fired Terry thought, but first things first.

Jackie Boy tells Terry not to worry after he finishes what he's come to say to Terry he won't be. Jackie Boy then tells Terry that he wasn't going to be working the club anymore and neither was the girl. Terry looks at Jackie Boy for a minute and then decides to throw some shade back at Jackie Boy telling him he didn't give a fuck what Jackie did but that the girl was staying as she was simply too valuable a money earner to just let go. Terry's looking fairly smug about his proclamation too as he stares across his desk at Jackie Boy like he's daring him to do something.

Jackie Boy had expected that Terry would try something considering the bravado the man carried about him without the weight to put behind it or carry it off. It was the man's fatal flaw to be unaware of this latter fact. What he didn't expect was that Terry would then double down on his bravado and dare a provocation again especially in the absence of any security near him or even Sissy to drag Jackie away from him this time.

Jackie Boy steps forward towards the desk noting that Terry hasn't taken any action to keep the separation between them the same not that he had any room to go in the cramped office. Terry about to get a lesson on the perils of false bravado as Jackie's hand shoots out from his side to grab Terry's injured hand as he brings his other fist down hard on the other hand and grinds it into the fingers eliciting a scream from Terry.

"Damn that's gotta hurt," Jackie Boy says to Terry when there's a pause in the man's screaming. Terry starts cursing Jackie Boy and issuing idle threats like he'd uttered to Jackie Boy once before about regretting this. How he didn't know who he was messing with and that Jackie Boy was one stupid mother fucker if he didn't understand that. Jackie Boy replies with another smash of Terry's hands and then asks Terry if he wants Jackie Boy to break the other hand.

Terry shakes his head no once he gets done screaming and has descended into feeling sorry for himself. "Then we're done here," Jackie Boy says. "The girl too you understand." Jackie Boy says as he finally releases the pressure off Terry's hand.

"Glad we had this talk then," Jackie Boy says as he straightens himself up and then walks out of the cramped office with a shout from Terry to go fuck himself. The thrown after him comment only makes Jackie Boy smile as he heads down the stairs and out of the club.

Terry takes a moment to suck up his pain while scrambling to first locate and then to uncap the pharmacy bottle of pain pills. He fumbles the bottle and scatters pills all over his desk and to distant corners of the office never to be recovered while uttering a frustrated fuck out loud. He pops two of the pills into in his mouth and chases them down with a swig from the glass of vodka on his desk which has amazingly made it through the encounter unspilled.

Terry then reaches for his phone and makes a call thinking to himself how this stupid mother fucker has made his last mistake.

King and Bones

Joey Bones hangs his phone up after the brief call from Terry down at the club where the trouble had first started. Joey's surprised that the hero had returned to rekindle those same troubles. He's a bit disappointed that the pair of cops which King had in his pocket hadn't been able to adequately dissuade the hero away and now he was going to have to deal with it himself. Dealing with it himself was not such the problem as much as how now he was also going to have to tell King about the mess this hero had made at one of their more profitable establishments while also exposing Terry as incompetent in the process and giving Joey Bones another thing he was going to have to deal with there too.

Frankly it was an embarrassment that Joey Bones hadn't yet been able to dissuade the would be hero off his present course as he was expected to deal with these kinds of things as a matter of course as part of his job after all. He hates that he has to tell King about the hero now who was proving more resilient than priorly was assumed about him. Joey Bones would rather have almost any other task rather than having to bring this to King and admitting the initial failure with the persistent hero. Still King had to know about the hero as he'd made too much noise to be ignored now with the disruption to their profits.

This was the gist of the unpleasant and mostly one sided conversation Joey Bones was presently having with King. They were in King's personal place located way Uptown somewhere off a stretch of Tchoupitoulas. They were within the spaces of his office and far from the source of most of King's income and business' by necessity and design. King was after all a respectable business man. Looking like a regular pillar of the community, provided you didn't look too close at him, and if you did, well, then there was Joey Bones to help you unsee it.

King's impeccably dressed in a cream colored suit which is well-tailored for his broad shoulders and the ubiquitous pistol in a shoulder rig beneath his coat. The coat was over a dark merlot colored shirt with an even darker merlot colored tie to compliment it. Joey only knows the color is merlot because King corrects him if he calls it by any other color's name. King sports a sharp and well-groomed goatee, but his most striking aspect in every sense which can be applied with the word, are his intense dark blue eyes which pierce right through you when he deigns to look right at you.

"We got ourselves a hero," Bones begins without preamble as he's stands before King, "goes by the name of Jackie Boy,"

"I'm sorry we've got what now," King asks Joey unsure he has heard what Bones has said to him correctly.

"A hero," Bones says again, "they call him Jackie Boy, or it's what he's called by most everyone. No last name either, just the sentence like it's the whole damn thing."

"Please tell me we know more about him than this," King dictates to Joey who never averts his eyes when speaking to King which he has always liked about Joey Bones and always had as opposed to his typical sycophants who were all too chickenshit by comparison.

"Not much more," Joey responds with a shrug and a short story to tell. "He's a knock around kind guy, poppin' up here and there but nothing noteworthy really. He does a lot of side jobs and knows a bunch of people throughout the Quarter and has worked both sides of the aisle but nothing big, nothing which would get a guy noticed and I think he prefers it this way."

A consternated King rubs his temples as if fighting off a headache, an apt description were it a little far north of the actual location this character was a pain in. He's not pleased that they know so little about a man who wanted to play hero and had disrupted one of their more stable and profitable establishments. He utters out a short 'fuck,' out loud, a rare curse used by King as his frustration was showing.

"Do we know anything more about this hero," King asks as he pours himself a drink and then sits back in his chair.

"Just stories," Joey finally says after a short while and King looks up from behind his heavily ringed hand to peek an accusatory eye to stab out in his patented death stare at Joey in an effort to make him uncomfortable. It's an effort wasted on a man with the weight of the sheer number of fights fought over his career facing badder men than King. He'd never let on mind you, but to a certain extent Joey Bones had lost the capacity to experience fear having built up a certain immunity to it. He found a comfort in knowing there wasn't much use for all of it fear because one way or the other everybody ends up dead and there really isn't much use in worrying a whole hell of a lot about it.

"What kinds of stories Joey," King finally asks exhausted at the silence offered up by his street commander Joey Bones which had lingered a bit too long for his comfort. Joey Bones looks up at him and shrugs his shoulders as he tells King how they're just stories with no way of knowing if there's any truth behind them or not.

"Tell them to me anyway Joey," King says with a wave of his hand in the classic give me more motion.

"He supposedly did a stint in the army," Bones says.

"And we know this because," King asks Joey getting a headache from having to exert all of this effort to pull the information out of Joey.

"He's got an airborne tattoo high up on his shoulder," Joey says, like this is the clearly obvious explanation of the conclusion reached. King shoots Joey a 'you've got to be kidding me' look which Joey ignores as he continues on with his short list of what will turn out to be some form of twisted tale passing itself as some form of personal history.

"There are rumors how he used to be NOPD but got his ass canned from the force right before Katrina, something about a stolen cruiser, a hooker and a hotel in Biloxi."

This story piques King's interest because it was pretty damn hard to get one's ass booted off NOPD after all. He decides this asshole managed it because what he'd done had been out of state which would have made it awful hard to cover it up considering the distance involved. It was a most impressive screw up King thought, even if only part of it was true and unable to separate that from the parts which are untrue considering how the whole story was fantastical.

"Those are interesting stories for just being rumors," King says as he looks up and over to Joey Bones who has stayed standing this entire conversation.

"Yeah," Joey says, "just rumors. There are no records to find on this guy anywhere. Our man inside said they all got washed away in the storm and this Jackie character used the opportunity to drop off the grid and had managed to stay off since this."

"Until now," King says.

"Yea, until know," Joey replies, "The man's been nothing but a ghost for years."

King contemplates the steaming pile which Joey has just shoveled over on to his desk as he attempts to focus on a solution to this would be hero problem called Jackie Boy.

"So maybe a badge and maybe not, and nothing we can offer him then," King says about the conundrum they faced as Joey's face pinches up in brief confusion.

"I assume you've already tried sending our pet cops out to help this man see the error of his ways," King says to Joey Bones who nods his head in the affirmative while leaving King hanging for a moment with the brevity of his reply. King finally looks at Joey Bones and asks him, and…?

"It didn't dissuade him," Joey Bones says.

"Well damn Joey, just what the hell am I supposed to do about this mess you just dropped in my lap," said King. He'd used the strongest curse he allowed himself to show his seriousness on the issue. King generally only rarely cursed as he thought cursing was the province of weaker and lower men and never would deign to stoop to blasphemy in any form. King considered it a form of separation between himself and people like Joey, who never did take it personally.

"I don't know," Joey says.

"This is just exactly what I have you around for you know," King flat tells him in an undisguised tone of displeasure.

"I know," Joey says offering no argument, such was his way. Joey Bones might be a simple soul, he might not be so smart and still he was an impenetrable cypher much to King's irritation. He never did get a solid sense of what Joey Bones was thinking or feeling at any moment in time.

"Well thanks then," and the sarcasm drips from King as he sits restless behind his desk hand in front of his face, fingers at the alternate ends of the bridge of his eyebrows.

"Damn," King said slamming his fist against the bookshelf cursing out a line of damns to follow after the first. King seethes with an anger which he's trying hard to get in front of, to prevent an interruption of his thought process, but he's too damned mad at Joey for his inability to solve what should be simple problem. His anger with Joey rising raised upwards now by the dropping of this clusterfuck into his lap when he reaches a decision. His theory is premised on the question of, if Joey cannot handle this would be hero, then there is but one recourse for King to take, however unpleasant the thought of it is and the shudders it causes simply from the thought of it.

King had taken his moniker and modeled his style based on an old Christopher Walken movie he'd seen one late at night a thousand years or so ago. He didn't exactly remember the plot, just a young Lawrence Fishburne and Wesley Snipes starring in it too. He remembered how smooth and fucking bad ass Walken was in it as he works to be the only crime lord in town. He thought about this movie as he contemplated how Walken himself would handle this situation knowing the man wasn't afraid to get his own hands dirty and blow the motherfucker away himself.

That was the way King envisioned it when an entirely different idea rose to the front of his brain. King thinking of Walken high up in his suite damn near the top of the world with his crew, his women, and a gun in his waistband with a plan in mind and how the man would appreciate this one too.

"Our hero hasn't seemed to be dissuaded," Joey Bones says earning a look of pure you've got to be shitting me from King.

"The damn man doesn't seem to learn anything then," King says and Joey leaves the self-evident statement where it lies having learned from long experience with King about the perils of extrapolating further than he was allowed to.

"There must be something we can do," King says as he rises to pace his office, "there must be something this hero wants."

"There's the girl then," Joey says in a pure stream of conscious extemporaneous moment unable to understand the implications of what he's said at first. Joey unable to hear what he's just said or suggested by its vocalization.

"Exactly," King says at first surprised somewhat by the direction being taken in the conversation as he mulls it over.

"Right," King says, "the girl."

"The girl then," Joey says this time less sure, wary of what has been started in motion.

"Exactly," King says a small grin on his face with the resolution to their Jackie Boy problem seemingly in hand, "We'll hit him in his heart."

Luxuries

Jackie Boy leaves the club feeling he'd done a good job of communicating with Terry about how neither he nor the girl would be his concern anymore. He heads through the Quarter going to see Sissy at her little cottage on Burgundy to tell her what he's done for them. He arrives on her doorstep and raps out a quick rat-a-tat-tat on it and then waits for Sissy to come to the door.

A form appears on the other side of the glass of the door appearing only as outlined shadow until it's lost when it lines up right on the other side of the door. He hears a muffled query of who is it is passed through the door which Jackie Boy answers by stating it was him. He hears the click of the deadbolt being unlocked and the turn of the doorknob before the door opens with the person answering it still behind the door. Jackie Boy's uncertain about entering until Sissy's head pops out from the other side and her hand and voice tell him to hurry his ass up and get in the house.

He follows her upstairs and watches her as she climbs into her bed mildly complaining that he'd left her and how it still felt awfully early in the day despite how it was already past lunch and on its way to dinner. Jackie Boy stokes her head as he sits in the bed next to her hardly able to contain himself with the news he wants to share with her.

"Something to tell you," he says to her and she sleepily replies what unprepared for the impact of what he's going to say. He then goes on to tell her how she doesn't have to go back to the club because he took care of it with Terry. She bolts upright in her bed her forehead scrunched up in clear anger as she spits venom at him.

It starts with how dare you Jackie, you'd better not have fucked that job up for me. It's not your place to be deciding things for me Jackie! You and your damned hero shit Jackie I'm sick of it she says as she drills a punch into his shoulder before she folds into herself with her arms crossed muttering things written in the language of anger.

Jackie feels he needs to explain himself to her, to explain his reasoning for the decision he'd made for the both of them. He realized now how he should have told her he was going to do what he'd already done. He wants to tell her how he feels, even though it's fairly clear this is not the time for it now, not when they're in the middle of an argument. Jackie, as is his nature, plunges ahead and offers the words out loud to her as his defense for the action taken.

The words said are met with silence and the display of the frown which sinks into her features as she shows her obvious displeasure with his choice made. She'd known what Jackie had wanted to say and had tried to cut him off before he could say it out loud. She hadn't wanted the word said or thought, hadn't wanted the word put out there where the whole world could know it.

She doesn't want it, the one word Ol' Jackie Boy has dared to utter which neither of them should be using. Jackie's saying of the word to her unheeding of the silent clues demanding against it being said was now forcing the issue unfairly she thought. A decisions coming, is being made, she decides and he's not certain he'll like the outcome.

"Dammit Jackie, you shouldn't have said that," she says past a brief pout before getting up from the bed and moving away from him to across the room. She turns her back to him so he cannot see her expression so he'll have to rely on reading her body language as the light flickers against her skin as she stands near the window. Her signals of anger and displeasure are clear in her expression but Jackie swears he sees a moment of sadness and loneliness there in her as well, unless he was projecting.

"You should know better than that Jackie," she says interrupting the prolonged pause with a deep sigh. Jackie Boy's not following her though because he got lost on one of the twists and turns in a scene he'd thought was going to play out very differently. Sissy can see he's lost, briefly thinks to herself he's hopeless and then chastises herself for the negative thought. She'd explain it to him if she could but she doesn't have the breath or time for it, let alone the words to sink through his thick skull when it should have been obvious from the start.

"Don't make me explain it Jackie," she says choosing the shorter course as she moves back to sit next to him, her arms are crossed tight against her torso closing herself off from him now and shutting down.

"You should know that's a luxury which we cannot afford to indulge in," she says to him. If Jackie was confused before, this word choice throws him off the ride entirely when she utters the word luxury out loud and is rewarded with a hard stare from Sissy.

"Yes," she says in a condescending tone, "A luxury, and one that isn't for us Jackie, for either of us. It's something which doesn't fit the situation or suit us at all."

"Sissy," Jackie says his tone filled with confusion and a bit of hurt before his thoughts trail away from him leaving him at a loss to fill in the space with words. Sissy is suddenly filled with remorse over what she has said but knows she must complete the circuit.

"Don't think it Jackie, don't ever say it again and maybe, just maybe we'll be ok," she states in a succinct and tight tone of voice. She looks away from him unable to witness the hurt it causes him to hear it and possibly to hide the same feeling from him. She doesn't like having to say these things or to utter words she never thought she'd have to phrase or coin. She eventually turns back to him as they stare our across a widening gulf growing between them which can never be spanned.

She reaches out a hesitant hand towards him wondering if he'll reach back for it briefly afraid he won't. He does and they fall into bed together lost in each other's bodies for the moment as he whispers apologies to her for what he had done and not understanding what was going on. The next day comes and they awkwardly separate and head in opposite directions with neither of them knowing if these directions will ever intersect again.

pages from the girl's diary

Charlie cannot believe this Jackie Boy and what he had done, first with the job and then with taking the liberty to express things which neither one of them should state let alone consider. It wasn't for them she thought and she cannot believe he'd say it out loud never mind the whole feeling of it which she herself wasn't so clear on so how could he possibly be so? She always thought of that kind of a thing as a fiction written for other people and properly categorized under falseness, or it might as well have been.

Charlie could have lived the rest of her life without this *intrusion,* this inconvenience unwanted and most importantly and appropriately, *undesired.*

She'd been doing fine out on her own, more or less in this low key low pressure life where no one was given to know her name let alone who she was. She preferred it to be this way which is why she'd chosen it after all.

And then this, this Jackie Boy coming to crash into her with the hero shit he insisted on clinging to. She wanted to maintain her distance and against her own devices, her own desires, wants and demands, she's finding herself drawn to the stupid schmuck. Charlie sighs then, a long and deep sigh, venting confusion and frustration at their situation.

Damn this attraction she curses when she realizes she's been masturbating almost unselfconsciously because she'd been thinking of him. She's and a little embarrassed by it as she sits on the couch, a reminder to her how attraction has no laws to guide it, bind it, thwart it or deter it which leaves her cursing herself for falling and realizing she was.

She's still mad at him for deciding she should quit the club and doing the quitting for her. He's clearly overstepped the line on that mark. She only hoped it wasn't too late and she could talk Terry into taking her back deciding she'll go to the club later to do just that.

Piece of Heart

Sissy goes back to the club to talk to Terry and it goes as she'd hoped it would. Terry tells her that there's no hard feelings between them as far as he's concerned. Not after she'd explained how Jackie boy didn't speak for her with Terry how he hadn't thought so and he was glad to have her back while asking if she was ready to work this evening. She replies that she can and he smiles a wide smile hiding his disingenuous nature saying to her good, now go to work. He waits til she leaves the room before he picks up the phone and makes a call.

Sissy finds she's a bit nervous to be back at the club without really knowing why unless it was because she hadn't told Jackie Boy she was going back. It wasn't his business anyway what she did. They had no hold on each other as she herself had so recently indicated and proven with her return to the club this evening. This evening was going to be just a normal night for her as far as she was concerned as she pushes thoughts of Jackie Boy far from her mind.

Her evening goes about as she expects until it picks up with the arrival of a pair of men who come into the club. They look like every other type of customer when they walk in, spending money to get noticed. It's an easy trick to pull in a strip *ahem* *gentleman's* club. They know what they're looking for and can get it easily with a quick flash of cash and all the other girls are disappointed when they select Sissy and Sissy alone for their little party. They order up a private room and dance and she takes them upstairs to a room at the front of the club which has a window out to the balcony and the street below like they'd requested. She moves to close the curtains, preferring the dark when she feels a large presence behind her. They offer no explanation or chance at all for her.

"I'll be right there baby," she says with a smile, "just sit down and relax,"

There's no response just the pressure of hands upon her shoulders and a forced movement forward.

There's a scream and then gravity.

The scene is being shot from above. There's the spiral of the camera outwards from the beginning with a tight focus on a bit of lace at a girl's thigh. Its white lace of course as she always wore white stockings topped with white lace when she danced. She's not dancing now, she lies instead smashed in the street. Broken like a crooked giant 'X' deformed and splayed out in the unforgiving street with a light rain splashing into her open eyes staring off into nothing. Her blondish hair is now turned to a strawberry blonde, a color choice she'd always spoke about having done minus the expense of her life's blood.

She'd been thrown from a balcony and it was just all so completely unnecessary. She was just a little girl. The only thing she'd had to do with any of this was Jackie

Boy. It left little doubt as to where to lay the blame for it all, where to point the finger.

Jackie had gotten to the scene too late to be allowed through the police lines and too late to make any claim upon her. Not that he had any claim to make or could without also compromising his own status and turning it into the one most wanted for questioning by the police.

He turned away from the street scene and into a drinking binge for a little while. He then tried not drinking at all but it only pushed him towards going straight strung out crazy, as if he was uncertain he wasn't already there and needed some kind of proof. He slipped into a deep wallowing pity, a dark depression and none of it helped him with the loss suffered. He cannot get it out of his head, cannot stop seeing her there in the streets all broken. Jackie Boy left with the question of why. Why would someone want to do something to a sweet, sweet girl who'd never done anything to anybody, never bothered a soul. The girl just another nobody like him.

Last Goodbye

The funeral scene is lifted right out from the past like something an old vision complete with carriage and coffin. One last ride through the Quarter and to a final destination Uptown into the Garden District and Lafayette Cemetery. He watches from afar, doesn't dare get too close seeming to instinctively know where he does not belong and yet he felt compelled to be here to at least be close.

She'd come from some money and now that money was paying to bring her back home. No one had known anything of it at all, no one had ever suspected. The term 'some money' is a quaint euphemism to disguise and obfuscate actual facts as no one's ever going to actually tell you in so many dollars and cents the actual figure but you can tell it's a substantial sum, a number too big to actually accurately depict.

Charlene Fanchon is the name which she'll be buried under. Fanchon, the family name was one with a long history in the areas of Southern Louisiana. Fanchon is a long storied name with a history of storied money behind it and half the parish in their employ and one quarter of all the best properties. The family name can trace its way back to before the Civil War. Hell to before Louisiana was part of the States and flew under a different nation's flag.

Sissy, as Jackie had known her and thought of her still, would have been a true southern belle if she'd stuck to the family plan. A plan which her stripping was certainly not included in. Good girls do not take off their clothes for money after all.

Jackie stands in front of the monument with the family name on the front after everyone else has left the cemetery. He stares at the fresh brickwork which is still wet and unsettled. He doesn't know if he should be here, feels like it is somehow sacrilegious or improper or unwarranted. An unacceptability if he just knew to whom or why.

No ceremonies for him as he would not intrude on the proceedings, or her family. He has have never been more aware of his standing as an outsider here and an unwanted one at that should he appear. Just another grim reminder of where their beloved daughter went wrong. It doesn't mean he's without a place here, it just means it would not be understood by the people who populate an entirely different world than he does, then she had, these people who call themselves her family.

He finds himself wishing for rain without knowing why other than it seems like it should be raining. The skies should be crying over the loss, it should always rain at a funeral. The sky and the world are uncaring though and do not note such trivialities. There's nothing but sun to fall upon him when inside him it's dark and cold filled with enough of each to drown a soul.

He stands in front of the fresh sealed oven uncertain as to any grasp to the why of his being here. He has nothing to offer here to the silent stone, no flowers or prayers or words to speak out loud. A brief moment passing where he wonders which of the two of them he's here for, a selfish moment, a wallowing moment which he doesn't allow to linger fearing it would be disrespectful to the dead all around him as well as her. He reaches into his pocket and pulls out two large coins and looks down at them in his hands before a long sigh escapes him. He looks about him left and right before he places the coins on the edifice near her freshly carved name. Two coins is the customary cost for the journey across to the next world. Jackie turns to walk away with two coins of his own clutched in his hand deep in his own pocket.

Jackie's briefly wondering how it had gotten here to this without bothering to look for the spot where it all went wrong. He knew it would be futile and a critique which people often made when they went looking for the pivotal moment when there was none to be had. Jackie Boy thinks even this is inaccurate as he knows how the pivotal moment can only be looked at in retrospect because in the moment it passes by unrecognized for the significance it will gain later.

All of those little moments an inch or two this way or not, are the places where it went wrong and all so innocuously too. Done without knowing or seeing how it's where it had started and where it had proceeded. Knocking along until suddenly you realize you're not even on the road anymore and by then, of course, it is way too fucking late.

Innocuous is how it starts, how it happens and without any intentions or thoughts. Just playing things out as they're occurring, hoping for the best when possibly one should've been exerting a little more control over the events as opposed to just sitting back and enjoying the ride.

Searching for Answers

When Jackie Boy finally climbs out of the bottle he realizes in a brief moment of clarity that somebody knows something about what happened to the girl. Somebody sold him out using her and most importantly somebody got paid to do it. Maybe multiple somebodies to give Jackie Boy a good place to start on the list of somebody's knowing who and more importantly right where they'd be. His first stop on the list is the asshole manager Terry at the strip club, pardon, *gentlemen's* club where the girl had last been.

The *ahem* *gentlemen's* club and Terry being, really, the only common link between Jackie and the girl which marked Terry as a most likely culprit in Jackie Boy's own mind. Terry was already known to be susceptible and willing to a number of underhanded behaviors. Tag on the animosity Terry felt towards Jackie Boy from the beginning where he and Jackie Boy had not gotten off on a good footing. Throw in how Terry had already shown a propensity towards being a generally dishonest person too and Jackie presumed Terry would not be against the idea of turning the girl out to interests concerned with hurting Jackie Boy after all.

Jackie Boy heads to the club in the short hours before the club opened proper brushing past the security on scene and pounding up the stairs to Terry's cramped office. He's ignoring the way this scene last played out as today Jackie Boy is prepared to deal out violence in direct proportion to the pain he felt over the loss of the girl. Jackie was a man with nothing to lose but pain in buckets to share and in a giving mood.

There's a girl on her knees blowing Terry when Jackie Boy bursts into the tiny claustrophobic room staring hate at Terry. "HEY," Terry shouts as he quickly attempts to sort himself and the girl out. Jackie Boy pauses to let the girl leave before he started up on Terry.

Terry's feeling chesty and a bit uncooperative opening his defense with a 'what the fuck are you doing here,' statement as he tried to rise to confront Jackie Boy. Jackie Boy shoves him back down into his chair while planting the heel of his booted foot in Terry's groin area noticing how in his haste how the damn fool had forgotten to zip up. Jackie doesn't pause as he asks Terry the simple question of who had he told.

Terry doesn't respond and unfortunately for him Jackie Boy's not in a negotiating mood while also feeling pressed for time. Jackie grabs Terry's right arm and hand and shoves them into a slightly open drawer of the desk which he then slams against Terry's fingers until he's rewarded with a satisfactory scream and crunch when Terry's fingers break. Jackie then squeezes them in his hands when he doesn't feel Terry's being on the complete up and up with him.

"You're cock is next Terry," he says, "So start talking."

Terry clearly believes Jackie Boy's threat as he gives Jackie Boy the name Joey Bones as the person he'd told. Jackie had only a limited knowledge of the name and all of it attributed to a guy who used to box in fights along the Gulf Coast circuit some years ago. Otherwise it doesn't mean anything to him, but maybe Bobby D would know which works out alright as Bobby D was Jackie's next stop anyway.

Jackie leaves with Terry behind him holding his crushed hand shouting out the usual warnings required here. Shouts of how Jackie Boy was going to regret this, how he'll never live through it. How he didn't know who he was messing with and then Terry completed it with the most common one leveled against Jackie Boy about how he is without a doubt one stupid mother fucker. Jackie Boy wasn't worried about the threats which felt mostly hollow. Besides, what's one more when you've already got a pile of them.

Jackie's next stop is Uptown where he storms into Bobby D's office and doesn't pause before throwing a punch at him landing square in Bobby D's face. The punch knocks Bobby D straight out of his chair and onto his lying ass against the wall to dribble in a heap on the floor partially upright from the same said wall.

"Damn Bobby! What you couldn't warn a brother or something," Jack shouts to which Bobby just shrugs his shoulders as he sits up from the pile on the floor he'd made. He's dressed in a bright multi-colored paisley shirt this time with the same wide collar and open to reveal both hair and the gold necklace buried within.

He wore blue bell bottom jeans with flowers at the bells and probably hand sewn into the bells which spoke of being vintage quality straight from the decade. There's a new splash of color red which Jackie can see from the splattered nose courtesy of the punch thrown as Bobby D sits with blood in his hand and wiped on the front of his shirt which wasn't going to ever be coming out from.

"Dammit Bobby!" Jackie shouts further.

"Fuck you Jackie," Bobby D shouts back at him.

"Did you really have to go and piss of King of all people you stupid mother fucker, shit," Bobby D continues to exclaim shaking his head at the depths which Jackie was able to sink his stupid ass down to while also threatening to take Bobby D down along with him on that ride.

"Your boy Terry sold her ass out," he says, "and that poor girl never did anything to anyone."

"You leave him alive Jackie." Bobby D says followed by a long pause before Jackie answers yeah he had and surprised to see how Bobby D actually seems relieved with the news.

"Thanks for that man, it would have broken my sister's heart otherwise," Jackie Boy looks over at him and Bobby D can read the 'c'mon man' written there in the expression, Jackie still smoldering at the contention.

"Whatta you going to do man," Bobby D says shrugging his shoulders, "it's my sister's kid and all that, and I said I'd look out for him. You know how it is."

"Yea and doing a fuck of a job with it too there Bobby," Jackie says, "too bad he's a waste of breathable air."

"Damn Jackie that's a little harsh especially coming from you," Bobby D says. The man has a point though which brings them both to a halt here. It's probably for the best before either of them says something, anything which cannot be taken back.

Bobby D's looking at Jackie Boy who's stuck a tick wondering what to do next. This being as far as Jackie's initial plan had carried him to and he doesn't quite know what to do next. Bobby D and him had tread a lot of ground over the many years stretching back into parts which are no longer able to, quite frankly, be recalled clearly and are better left that way of a whole lot of reasons. So there was no reason to take things any farther unless he was prepared to trash all of that.

"Damn if that aint some sad old bullshit story you fuck," Jackie Boy says to Bobby D, who's disgusted at the thought of the family relation which had put him in this situation.

"Sorry man," Bobby D says, "but it's the truth." Jackie Boy stares hard at him lying there. Jackie's still mad as hell but also thinking of all the miles which he and this man have under their feet all of these years of knowing each other. He's working on deciding whether to throw all that away and over a worthless fuck like Terry too.

"What in the fuck are you so pissed the fuck off for anyway Jackie," Bobby D demands, leaving Jackie stumbling for an answer. He's working his jaw trying to come up with a response. He's feeling it should be ready made or at least at the tip of his tongue and readily accessible but nothing comes at first. Then everything builds behind the blockage, threatening to landslide out in an unflattering burst of incoherency.

"Loved that little girl," Jackie Boy finally says in a whisper, a whisper feels appropriate, leaving Bobby D here perplexed at the words coming from Ol' Jackie Boy's mouth like he'd just spouted Ovid in the original Latin.

"Man," Bobby D says stretching out the word like a long sigh, "Jackie we've known each other a long, long time now right?" To which Jackie nods in the affirmative.

"You sure you got that right there Jackie?" Bobby D asks him and Jackie arches an eyebrow at him.

"What," Jackie says back to him like he's been stunned or something. "You think I don't know about those kinds of things?"

"No Jackie, I don't," Bobby D says being as blunt as only a longtime friend such as Bobby D is can be.

"No Jackie, It's not that," Bobby D says, "it's just not possible for all kinds of reasons. It's not something you're capable of having."

It's an unvarnished and painful truth which pisses Jackie Boy off as he stares hard at Bobby D as his hands form fists. Jackie can feel his anger rising to a boil and turning his face red. He stares hard at Bobby D as he works over a debate about all their shared miles.

"Whoa Jackie, calm down now there," Bobby D says as he puts his hands into the air in the classic I surrender, mean no harm pose asking Jackie Boy who keeps his stare fixed on Bobby D. Jackie's contemplating things though he's uncertain how it has come to this or just what plan he'd just so shortly ago envisioned. His slogged in brain is working at the dilemma which offered no clear routes away from, no clear ways for him to go and no relief offered.

"What man," Bobby D, "what do you want from me Jackie," but Jackie doesn't have an answer.

"Aw fuck it man," Jackie says and walks out of Bobby D's office with no destination in mind.

Dead Man's Town

King had left the hero problem to Joey Bones to take care of knowing that Joey Bones had no choice now but to handle the situation personally. Joey Bones had agreed with the sentiment and King had sent him off telling Joey how he just wanted to be kept informed on what had been going on. King's thinking Joey could have led with that as Joey leaves King to his brooding and his whiskey.

King's still a little pissed with Joey Bones for letting it get this far with the hero without stepping into to stop it earlier despite knowing he'd correct the error this very evening. A damned hero was the last thing King needed and this stupid son of a bitch who wouldn't listen to reason gave King a headache of a kind he hadn't suffered in years. He grabs his glass of whiskey and takes a god jolt from it before he raises it into the air in a silent toast or prayer to Joey Bones' success tonight.

Jackie Boy's walking through the Quarter cutting through the alley next to the cathedral when he's knocked flat on his ass once more with a blow from out of nowhere. The blows don't even think about abating until he's down on all fours and then they only slow to a lesser beat. He hears another set of steps walk up to him past the two shadows flanking him into his present position. He hears the distinctive click of metal indicating a pistol which had been cocked and he assumes is, or soon will be, pointed at him.

Jackie Boy's looking down and trying to regain his focus thinking when he does about the street he's looking at. The street has old blood in the ground beneath these pavers in the square, old and ancient blood going back who knows how far when. They used to do hangings here along with executions and other punishments back when the city was still part of a foreign empire. Blood in the ground beneath the pavers is a certainty if not also in the pavers themselves as well. No telling how deep or soaked the ground might actually be with it, though it's probably part of the reason the park is so pretty. Wild things always grow better with blood in the ground.

"Jackie Boy," the man who walked up with the gun in his hand now says his name like a question. "Are you listening to me?"

Jackie offers no response to the man as he was a little preoccupied trying to ignore all the pain he was presently in, not mentioning the about to be shot portion of the event.

"You've done good and fucked up now Jackie," says the man with the gun. It's a rather blatant statement of the obvious for how else does one end up in the position which Ol' Jackie Boy found he was in currently.

"You're one stupid fuck motherfucker do you know that," continued the voice in more obvious exposition. "Sticking your damn nose in places where it's not wanted, and even after you'd been told to mind your own damn business."

Jackie wasn't certain but figured this asshole meant the girl as the reason for his present predicament. Then again, maybe Jackie was wishing this as the most likely reason for his present predicament. It was hard to say really, as Jackie had gotten himself about knee deep into at least three particular kinds of shit in the past few days, making it a skosh hard to tell just which one this specific asshole was possibly referencing here even if it was the girl who stood out most in Jackie's own thoughts now.

"Not you though, oh no, not you," the voice continued. Jackie Boy's thinking 'fuck this asshole' who liked to keep yammering on, Jackie wishing that he'd just get on with it already. Get to the point or get to the shooting unless his plan was to talk Jackie to death.

It's not to be though as the man with the gun pointed at Jackie's head rattles on prolonging the stupidity. Building the suspense is how it would be described in the side notes on the script page but all Jackie Boy can think about as he's staring into those pavers is his own blood splattered on them and the straight pure annoyance of the fucking history lesson from the asshole with the gun's waxing soliloquy. The gun unwavering at his head as Jackie once more wishing r the man to stop talking and just fucking shoot already.

The man's head turns looking down at Jackie Boy as if he's heard his thought process him to grant his wish.

"Dammit why don't you just die already," the gunman says, "it's all anyone wants from you anyway."

He pulls the trigger and the gun fires and Jackie's world ends in a very bright flash of nothing but pain followed by darkness falling fast and cold creeping in as the gun finally fires.

Jackie Boy had heard the metallic click of the big revolver cycling before he felt the bang of the slug as it punched into him. The shot so close to his head and near his ear so all he can hear now is some damn horrible ringing echoing about in his skull.

The bang replays over and over again interrupted by Jackie's cursing of the pain as he lies rolling in the street. He's not rolling so much as he's a crumpled mass of humanity lying face down in the bricks of the street, bricks which are feeling too cold for this tropical city. Jackie swears he can see his breath as it exits his mouth to scatter across the pavement in short grey puffs of shorter and shorter bursts til the last one slinks out across the stones and into the street at last.

Shivers

Jackie Boy's lying on the cold pavers of the street as the warmth of his body bleeds out into the cold street beneath him. He's waiting on another kick, actually praying for the next shot as it would put an end to all this stupidity, even if it's mostly his own. There will be plenty of time to reflect on this later in the expansive land of wherever he's going next, so there was no bother to dwell on it now. Jackie Boy's been getting kicked down so often, that staying down sounded like a particularly attractive option. He doesn't want to get up despite all the demands of his body screaming at him to do so even as the protestations are pounding a beat in his head to add to the cacophony of the echoing shot rattling around in the opposite direction.

Jackie feels a shadow cross over the spot he's occupying on the pavement sending a deep soul shiver through his body as he recognizes something very ancient and predatory has come across him. He hears an eerie tune being hummed and then the scuff of the man's shoes on the pavers next to Jackie Boy's body. He's surprised at both considering how sharp his hearing seemed now that he was dying.

The person standing over him shifts their weight as they crouch down next to his body sliding their hands underneath his face down form and effortlessly rolling him over on to his back. The man then leans in close to Jackie seeming to breathe in his scent or some crazy shit. Some weird assessment of Jackie Boy going for a long uncomfortable moment as if the man with the porkpie hat believes Jackie has something he wants.

Remarkably Jackie has enough sight left to see at least part of the man who'd been leaning over him and had now returned to standing. Jackie looks up to see a tall thin man in a porkpie hat and beautiful spun gold clothes whose face disappears into the swirls of a shadow not conceivably or possibly cast by the brim of the small hat he wore let alone at this hour of the night. The man's visage reminds Jackie Boy of the old saying which warned about speaking of the devil or he just might appear. Jackie thinking he just might be looking at the truth of the idiom as he looks over the man and his sudden appearance thinking that as descriptions go for that character, that man might just look like the person standing above him.

The man was tall and dark like a cliché but not so much until he was right up next to you when he seemed to suck the breath right up from out of your lungs. He was so very thin, that it made him seem so much taller, like skyscraper tall. The thin man was hard to make out more past that as he seemed surrounded by a dark like the soulless stretches of deserted space far from any city out on America's highways.

The man was smoking a small thin something which didn't smell like a cigarette or cigar but what Jackie imagined was what brimstone might smell like if he had it to compare to. The man seemed in no particular hurry as he stood completely at ease over our boy Jackie as if it was the most natural thing in the world for him to be there. Jackie tries to maneuver his body into a more dignified position when the thin man places his foot on his chest and pushes him back down easily despite Jackie's attempts at protestation against the power of a man who's far too strong.

The thin man stares off into a distance which seems unnatural, seeing things others dare not imagine. Jackie lies still beneath the man's well adorned foot counting his aches and pains. Jackie makes it from one through one hundred or so when the pressure is released and the thin man pulls the front of his trousers up to save their crease as he crouches down to Jackie. The ugly black twig of a faux cigarette's parting his thin lips before he pulls it away to smolder in his right hand at his knee as he blows a string of the noxious smoke into Jackie's face.

"Dead man," the thin man says out loud, his voice low and filled with a depth most voices can never find giving his voice a quality which didn't necessitate a volume other than the one he currently spoke at. Jackie's uncertain if the man's opening words are how he's addressing Jackie Boy or if they're the rather ominous and declarative pronouncement of his condition. Jackie Boy briefly has a moment between thinking of death and wondering what the fuck was going on to briefly entertain the idea of wanting to know who this thin man is except for how there are deep primitive parts of his mind screaming their advice against asking so blatantly stupid a question. You don't ask the devil for his card after all.

"Been looking for you dead man," the thin man says just leaving it hang there for a moment as he slowly and purposefully takes another drag from his cigarette. The thin man places the cigarette back between his lips only to have his hands immediately filled with an evil looking black knife carved, and carved is the word for it mind you, to look like a lick of flame.

Jackie Boy's very aware of a wicked long flame like black knife the man carries in his right hand as his left hand moves about Jackie's chest. The left hand suddenly grabs up a fistful of Jackie's shirt and the thin man is so damned strong he's able to lift Jackie off the ground only to drop him as the knife hand lashes out to slash his shirt apart, navel to chin.

Jackie lands with a hard crack back on the pavers with shooting stars flaring into existence in his eyes and brain. This pain is quickly ignored though, pardon, this pain *is* replaced with another more excruciating pain. The man takes to tear into Jackie Boy's shirt, using the tip of the blade to push the remnants of the shirt to Jackie's sides before returning the blade to his chest. The thin man uses his wicked looking black knife to carve, and again, there really is no other word for the activity, something into Jackie's chest.

The thin man centers the tip of the wicked looking knife's point just below his sternum and raises the blade perpendicular to ninety degrees in relation to Jackie's chest. The point of the flame anchors there for a moment of excruciating pain which is multiplied by the slicing of a very straight line over Jackie's heart. This slice is swiftly followed by another crosswise slice and both feel like a laser cutting through his body.

The thin man finishes with his preliminary work setting the wicked looking knife to the side for the moment to Jackie's relief. A relief which is short lived as the man then places his hands on either side of the new wound in Jackie's chest. His right hand forms into a knife like wedge and Jackie can see how sharply pointed the fingernails are on this hand. The thin man's left hand pries open the wound to provide entry for the right with its knife edge and pointed fingertips. They find purchase in his skin before beginning their descent into his chest by digging deep into his chest cavity.

Jackie's pretty sure he knows this isn't possible and he's delusionally seeing things and wouldn't believe it except for the pain and later, the faded scar as if the wound was already old. An extremely agonizing moment more passes which put the combined ones felt earlier into a perspective, which, seem no more than mere annoyances in comparison to the pain he was currently feeling now.

The thin man removes his hand from Jackie's chest, seemingly eating something out from the palm of his hand and licks the blood clean from his fingers finishing with something approximating satisfaction. The man laughs a low deep bass grumble of a laugh which most people if heard would describe and recognize as evil. Not Jackie though, he'd been way too close to it, to the man, to ever be so casual or flippant with such a non-descriptive word, such a word which cannot ever describe him cheapens him with its application.

Luckily the pain is at a level which prevents Jackie Boy from fully realizing the absolute horror of the scene he's in and mitigates his ability to be frightened. This thought is quickly disproved however when the thin man sets the blade aside and then drags his pointed and sharp fingernails into the groove created by the crossed wounds on his chest. The thin man raises his fingers up to his lips to lick them clean of Jackie's fresh blood. The thin man waits a moment deciding something before making a small slice into his own thumb and allowing his own precious blood to pool before he runs the bleeding digit through Jackie's wound to add to the excruciating pain Jackie was collecting. Finished, the thin man stands back up to his full towering height again in what looks like a satisfied pose. The knife is put away once more and the still burning cigarette is back between his lips.

"Dead man," the thin man says in a brief moment after Jackie's pain has cleared from Jackie and he can actually feel like he has the capability of seeing straight. Jackie has a flash of a more formal name for the thin man hovering above him. The name is Voodoo Man though Jackie doesn't know why he felt it was correct to call the man the name he'd chosen. It doesn't seem to anger or bother the thin man much though, so Jackie lets it slide as he goes back into the bliss of the darkness.

"I bring you back dead man," the thin man above him says bringing Jackie Boy back from where he'd been comfortably traveling. It's not quite the relief you'd think it would be for Jackie who was clearly expecting for there to be some sort of a catch to it or something near like it. Jackie wants to ask the man why but stops the plainly stupid question from ascending from his mouth when he realizes it was a question you should never ask of a person who has decided to spare your stupid, sorry ass.

"Living is more painful after all dead man," the thin man says like a man who knows what he's talking about while looking off into a far distance not matched by the view in front of his eyes.

"Time for vengeance now dead man," the thin man says to Jackie Boy who is still lying in the street. Jackie's not certain he's heard the thin man correctly but isn't going to get any clarification as the thin man smiles and then vanishes with a slight turn into the darkness startling the word fuck from Jackie Boy's lips.

The word fuck is still resonating in Jackie Boy's brain as he thinks how much he has always hated all this god damned spooky shit and the shivers it sent up and down his spine. He wants to question why the city self-proclaimed as most haunted feels the need to conjure up more spooky shit while wishing for a hard shot of whiskey or two or three to take the edge of this damn nightmare. The thin man was a straight scarier individual than Jackie Boy hopes to never make the acquaintance of that particular person though he doesn't think it would be possible to find any such an individual anyways.

Jack Kelly

The Dead Returned

Jackie feels an immense amount of pain which is strange as pain should not be felt if one's dead or this is his working theory at any rate. He's still gathering information on all fronts. It's not like he has any prior first-hand knowledge of this while being dead thing. He does have more than a working man's knowledge of pain. Call it a working familiarity with it. Not that it can help him with what he's experiencing here.

Surprised is what he is at finding himself down and bleeding in the streets if still breathing too. Startled a good word for it as well as he seems to find himself not dead and still on this rock. He's lying on the pavers of which he'd previously spoken about. He's watching as his blood seeps into and over them, watches as a rivulet rolls towards a crack in the pavers. He watches it until it reaches the edge of the paver and hovers there for an interminable amount of time. He swears he can see the rivulet of his own blood quiver for a second before it succumbs to gravity and falls into the crack to join the accumulated blood that lies here in this square and its surroundings, a merger with the world right as he's supposed to be leaving it.

But he's not yet at any rate. Something demands that he get up, that he stop this dicking around and get up. It's insistent to the point of pestering and nuisance and beyond ignoring even if he had the strength or notion to do so. He finds the smallest amount of strength to curse it, if mostly under his breath even as he begins to move to obey its commands. He finds a desire to gather enough strength to rail against it and then to drop away from the world, straight down dead just to get away from it all.

This brings a ragged laugh from him as he manages to raise himself up on all fours like a dog though this is insulting to dogs mind you. The insistence is telling him how it's nothing more than a damn *scratch*. The ragged laugh dislodges a clot of blood which rises up and into his mouth which he then hacks it out onto the pavers before he shortly follows it into the blackness.

The blackness is short lived as the demand to rise up continues pounding around on the inside of his skull like a major college drum line. Get up, the demand made but he doesn't want to comply. He's thinking he really doesn't want to get up cause fuck Christ it hurts. It hurts like no pain he has ever felt or dealt or known by proxy.

A flash of memory and Sissy is falling. She's always falling as he remembers her in a strange projection of events which Jackie himself had never seen in reality. It haunts him and threatens to take away all of the pleasant memories of her, wanting to rob away everything else about her.

It was a trick of memory though as it wasn't Sissy falling but him as he splatted against the pavers once more in a most undignified fashion. Luckily, it least had isn't so far a distance for him to all from his kneeling positon.

Get up now, the insistent demand comes, when he'd been thinking he was quite comfortable right here on the cold ground. It insists until a ragged breath escapes his tattered lips blowing more blood past his teeth. Trying he says the word like a protestation. He curses as he rolls to his side, he swears liberally as he rises to all fours again. Blasphemies and curses fall from his lips easily and carelessly unheeding of his proximity to holy ground or being out in public.

He reaches out with his right arm and hand to the wall he thinks is there. He finds it and uses it to offset his awkward rise up to kneeling. He sucks in a desperate breath of air into his lungs and past his tortured ribs. He dares to open one eye to orient himself as he sucks in another breath as he rises to one knee. He pauses as he sucks down another breath and holds it as he rises to his full height more or less own his wobbly and unstable legs and then expells the held breathe with a curse out into the night.

Jackie manages to shuffle his left foot forward an indeterminably short length forward following it with his right. He repeats the process maintaining some semblance of forward motion while smearing the wall with his bloody hand and shoulder. He's using the wall to mostly maintain his upright position his brain doing the painful calculations to the next point where he can repeat the process. He even briefly dares to attempt the math which will carry him all the way to the house of The Mistress. Presuming of course he can find it from here.

Jackie feels sick over the providence which has left him still here on this damn wreck of a rock, enough so to drive Jackie Boy first to his knees and then to all fours, and then to kneeling, moving to his first try at rising, to standing up. Fine, *leaning* against a wall more than standing but certainly qualifying as best case considering what had just transpired.

Jackie Boy's stumbling about with his head down, only able to see the immediate pavement before his toes and the swing of his arms as he shambles about like some form of frightening creature from myth or horror. His frazzled brain has only enough computing power to calculate the next step in a direction he already knows to go at this unsteady if consistent gait towards a destination.

He's seeing ghosts and other haunts as he walks though this is not such an unfamiliar or uncommon occurrence here in this city, though this is the first time he's seen them so clearly. They, for their part, do not seem to be particularly surprised to see him though. If he had any natural inclination or spare thought process this would strike him almost as the lesser of the shocks of his current condition. The alive and shuffling portion of, if generously stated here in this description, it's still the more surprising of the two and not the ghosts. Jackie Boy's spent way too much time, more time than he'd care to admit on either front deep in the Quarter at all kinds of after dark hours where all the spooky bump in the night things dwell, especially in this city most haunted.

Jackie's continued flirtation with, near and around death leaves makes conclusion more foregone than the simple certainty of born to die. It was mostly surprising it had taken Jackie and death this long to get together, though apparently taken didn't mean what it once did what with Jackie Boy walking around and what not.

Jackie Boy realizes this is some warped form of providence leaving him still alive somehow despite having been left for dead. He chastises the gunman for not making sure. Jackie would have made sure. He'd at least have shot more than once to ensure he'd be staying down for a good long time. This sentiment pretty much sums up how he's feeling about the, much to his surprise, discovery of life still within him. He briefly ponders over the how in the hell could this be, but doesn't want to linger on it for long as it only drives the pounding, blistering beat rapping around his skull.

It seems like so much impossibility his still being ambulatory, but then, it's most probably part and parcel with the definition of the word providence. Damn all of the gods, Jackie thinks, though not too loudly. Damn them or whatever has provided this pass because they've decided they're not done with him yet. He assumes it's because they must still find him too amusing to just let die.

The irony of the moment is not completely lost on our hero Ol' Jackie Boy despite the inability to focus his brain past the competing beats within his own skull. A phrase pops to the front of his brain for one horrible clarifying moment before back into the din. The phrase telling him how there's no shame in falling down. Shame only arrives in not getting back up. It feels pertinent, if annoying, as Jackie tries to rise up out of pure mule stubbornness versus any noble or clichéd phrases quoted. Plain stubbornness tinged with some outright anger from Jackie as his response to the unfair trade of his life for hers, or so it feels, or will mostly later as right now is mostly full on pain Jackie feels.

His eyes are only able to focus a very short distance ahead forcing him to look down at his feet, watching as they shuffle forward. It's a gracious description of the inch by inch grab of street with a lean against the wall as a crutch. Jackie Boy inching his way down the alleyway heading towards the glow on his right the time passing in what feels like hours or days, but he knows is only minutes into his journey.

Jackie stumbles into the distinctive bar on the corner, shuffles over to the bar and orders absinthe. He pulls himself into a form of standing against the bar behind which resides a very buxom waitress who seems to know him. She's dressed in attire more fit for the nineteenth century then whatever today is. She sets up his order in the traditional manner, complete with the flaming sugar cube and his second history lesson of the night. The green liqueur soothes the pain he feels or at least makes them distant to the touch and more pleasant to deal with.

Jackie pulls some bills out and leaves them on the top of the bar before he departs to resume his stumble to. He locks on to the destination he knows by instinct alone, which is good because it's all he's operating on presently. He heads down past Ursulines to the door of The Mistress, to darken it once more. Jackie has thoughts to let her read his mind or at least chase this damned persistently pounding headache hammering away in his head.

There'll be no hospitals for Ol' Jackie Boy as he heads deeper into the Quarter towards The Mistress' door in the hope she'll put him back together as she always has before. He's fortified with the knowledge how The Mistress' had an uncanny ability at putting him back into a semblance of a functioning, living breathing human being every time he'd gotten himself taken apart. Jackie doesn't know the means she uses, he simply knows she's never failed to put Jackie back into the fight no matter his condition upon arrival at her door and giving The Mistress plenty of practice, as she'd always told him before continuing on with the observation how Jackie had a singular penchant for getting himself into this condition.

The Mistress could see into the future, of this Jackie was certain despite her protestations to the contrary and her efforts at deflection honed to an expert level. She could see into the future if not always reliably, hence the caveats against heavy declarations which, in her defense, were only really made by others. The future is too prone to fluctuation providing too many shifting potentials to be accurately read and would be old news by the time it's been reported kind of phenomenon. Events on the ground as it were have outpaced the 'news, 'which was why The Mistress kept her own counsel on these matters.

Still, for all Jackie's belief in her ability to see into the future she seemed to have a particular blind spot when it came to him for whatever reason. He based this on how she always seemed surprised to see him whenever he'd found his way back to her door at odd and uncertain hours like the proverbial bad penny he seemed to be.

Jackie moves into parts of the Quarter which are always familiar no matter his condition when he passes by them. He knows he's making progress, even if it's tortuous progress towards her. The Mistress' house is like a beacon and his personal refuge without proper license or right to it and still, she always eventually lets him in. A theory he's about to put to serious test.

Jackie's head is still ringing so damn loud though Jackie lacks the ability to properly contextualize it. The throbbing pain makes him almost wish he'd previously concurred with the man with the gun when he'd decried Jackie's sentence earlier. Why don't you just die a good question indeed and something else which Jackie Boy hadn't been able to do despite its simplicity furthering the gunman's point of Jackie's continued streak of done good and fucked up now.

Jackie loses his concentration to his detriment as he stumbles up over the curb and trips past a post to slam into an unyielding wall. The impact throws all of his aches and hurts back into serious disarray which threatens to overwhelm his alarm system which was already at blinking red everywhere it could. He swallows down a scream cursing a long blue streak of the word fuck repeated a number of times in succession like it's a new mantra or some form of sick prayer to an especially hateful god who enjoyed the pain portion of the event.

Part III: Good Deeds

No good deed goes unpunished.

-Oscar Wilde

Remedy

Jackie Boy continues his stumble down to the Mistress' house down past Ursulines in the Quarter down to see if she's still willing to provide a cure for all that ails him presently. He has no idea of how he makes the trip or how long it must have taken until he arrives to bang on the familiar door until the Mistress answers. She appears in the doorway pissed beyond words at the intrusion at this hour. It's an expression which doesn't change when she recognizes the deliverer of this late night knocking who is standing in her doorway once more.

She steps back from Jackie collapsed in her doorway to allow him to fall farther into her entryway while she steps back inside. She looks him over a quick minute all business like and then she disappears into the interior of her house for a moment. She returns with a sheet of heavy plastic which she slips beneath him before leaning down and taking a good handful of his clothes at his shoulders to drag his heavy stupid ass into her front parlor for another practice round of doctor. She quickly gathers a number of items and things she's going to need to help him before she kneels down beside him on the floor and begins to work on him as he falls into unconsciousness.

He wakes to the feeling of a green fire which burns in his veins leaving a tinge at the peripheral of his narrowed vision. A long dark haired woman dressed entirely in black says something to him but he cannot understand the words said. He's stripped to the waist and bathed in sweat under which a variety of calligraphic marks inked in black and red are written upon his skin. The marks are as foreign to him in as many different definitions with which the word can be used. He presumes the marks are in Latin or some other damn dead language.

Jackie's fevered brain is trying to process the scene even though it has its hands full fighting to stay alive and should not be given over to any wanderings from the effort being made. He's burning he realizes, reaching degrees which should not be possible. He can feel the fever raging inside his skull to match the heat built up in his body.

The Mistress' cure seems clear to him, it's an attempt to burn out what threatens to overtake him. She brings a comfort when her hand reaches under his head and tries to raise it up to take a sip of cold water from the glass she holds in her hand. The relief is short lived and he's mildly surprised the water hasn't turned to steam from its contact with his fever. For that matter, he doesn't understand how The Mistress herself can manage before he sinks back down into the burning.

The Mistress is humming to him, working a prayer over him while working her magic into his skin with the markings and oils made by her own hands. Incense burns and he can smell the strains of something simmering on the stove which his fevered state turns into a witches brew from what he assumes is the classic witch's pot atop her stove filling her house with its aroma which had made its way to envelop him where he lies on her couch.

They stay like this for an indeterminate amount of time which is feeling very long to him despite his inability to actually tell or note the time passed in this alternative feverish unreality. The Mistress applies her potions and her medicines into Jackie Boy's skin and even manages to pour some delightfully warm soup into his mouth sending it speeding its way through his system down and around.

Hours pass, days pass and he's so lost he'll never really know the scope of time involved. He'll simply know the amount which he feels has gone. It feels like a drunk, the lost time, the lost memories before a few memories come screaming back in to be never forgotten in a smolder for him to tender and keep like a fire so it doesn't burn out. The smolder keeps the cold and the rain away leaving him determined to stoke it and build it up into a source for his anger so he can finish the course he's set on embarking upon. Vengeance is usually reserved for the gods and considered a most noble endeavor but then,

Jackie Boy frankly wasn't going to give a damn about any gods who would let happen what they had to Sissy.

He wakes on the Mistress' couch his entire body nude except for the thin blanket covering him and his cold sweat. The remnants of his fever burned out and now producing a chill upon his skin. He sits in the dark pretending he wasn't missing her like an old song, and probably more than one at that too.

He feels a pounding sound which he, at first, cannot trace back to a source until he realizes it's not external. It's in his own damn head rattling around in all of the open space there and increasing when he tries to sit up way too quickly and almost as quickly convinces him to currently do otherwise. He wisely accepts this thought as he reverses course to stay where he's. Jackie looks about him as the blanket he was under has slipped down to his waist to reveal that he's shirtless and naked minus the marks on his chest which haven't gone away. He realizes it's most likely that they won't any time soon and he finds a strange comfort in their inked forms imbuing his skin, The Mistress' mark upon him as he sallies forth.

"You should be dead," he hears her voice say out loud in a tone which has surprise writ in it. He makes the mistake of shaking his head because he wasn't certain if he'd heard her right but it sure seemed like she'd pronounced him dead. Then again, every word's coming through muddled and unclear as he's looking mostly at her floor trying to recover from the mistake of shaking his head to revive the pounding headache it contains while wishing for unconsciousness to rise back up to blissfully claim him.

"How you're not dead though is interesting because it certainly isn't from a lack of trying," the smooth voice tells him as she walks into the room with a tray in her hands. Jackie absentmindedly rubs his head and then asks the Mistress if she's sure he wasn't dead. She stares at him a minute disbelieving that he'd ask that question of her like she wouldn't no one way or the other considering her line of work.

"Could have sworn I'd gotten myself shot," Jackie says as he looks at the hand which had previously been rubbing his skull and finding an absence of bandages there.

"You did Jackie but there's no need to be so dramatic about it," she says to him. "The damn thing bounced right off your damn thick skull and while it hasn't done anything for your looks and you'll probably have quite the headache for some time. But you're not dead yet."

Jackie mumbles out the word fuck as he tries to recall the events of the other night. The memories are scarce on details of any kind except the pavers which Jackie Boy remembers looking at as his blood seeped into them. He remembers cold and then he recalls wicked pain in his chest and a tall thin apparition bent over him. He shouts out in a combination of fear and anger which rouses his headache up again to spike in pain against his skull until it drives him back down into the cushions beneath him.

Jackie pinches his nose at the bridge and fights off the headache as best he can as he remembers the thin man and how the man had taken something from him as he lay on the pavers. Jackie he examines his chest tearing at the careful dressings the Mistress had applied there to a wound he'd seriously hoped not to find there. Hoping against hope it was simply some kind of particularly vivid nightmare he'd experienced as opposed to the waking horror as evidenced by the real and now seeping wound lying across his heart directly.

He opens his eyes and sees The Mistress staring at him with concern asking him what had happened to him just then. Jackie waves her off for a moment asking for a glass of something to drink and waits til the Mistress returns with a short glass of whiskey. He tosses it back and then clears his throat before he even attempts to answer her silent question.

He tells her about being accosted, about the third man with the gun pointed at his head and of getting shot and lying there dying on the pavers. He knows it was dying, been too close to it a time or two before to not recognize it when it arrives to stay. He then goes on to describe the arrival of the thin man and his activity after his arrival. How Jackie Boy had thought of him as The Voodoo Man and ending with Jackie Boy's arrival on her doorstep like always.

Jackie had felt The Mistress stiffen her back next to him on the couch at the mention of the thin man like she was familiar with who he was talking about. Jackie wonders if that's fear there within her causing her to stiffen like she does, not that he can blame her for it or would. Having experienced the thin man for himself he felt that fear was an appropriate response to the man. A good healthy dose of fear next to caution and respect and a note to oneself to give the man a wide berth should he be encountered again.

The Mistress, in a voice recovering from being momentarily lost causing it to be minus its usual vibrancy, asks Jackie Boy if the thin man had told him anything after finishing his work with the blade. Jackie watches how her hands are shaking despite her efforts to hide them. It's subtle but still just enough to see it because of how out of the ordinary it was on The Mistress after all.

Jackie thinks about it for a moment sorting through incomplete and unsorted memories of an incident he'd rather not recall for the chief memory of the event is pain. Excruciating pain like he'd never felt before in his life. But through the pain there's something else, some thread which the thin man had left Jackie Boy with. He can just make it out there on the edges of all of the pain experienced and then he has it. The thin man had left Jackie Boy with an imploration to go and seek out his revenge.

The Mistress stares at Jackie Boy a minute as she begins to pack up her stuff and then stands as she busies herself with various busy work around her cottage. Jackie's left on her couch wondering what had just transpired. He was doubly worried by the fact that The Mistress seemed to know whom he'd been talking about and had seemed to know the thin man as well. It was worrisome leaving Jackie Boy wishing he had the words to begin to form the questions he felt were necessary but didn't wish to see the light of day.

Articulo Mortis

Jackie wakes up later on The Mistress couch wondering how long he'd been out this time. He attempts to rise and as promised the thumping inside his head doesn't go away but it hadn't while he slept and certainly hadn't now that he's awake. It takes a moment before he realizes another oddity of the situation. He's been left alone in The Mistress house. Truthfully, this freaks him out a little bit, he's never been left alone in her house before and he doesn't quite know what to make of this new development.

Fortunately he hears her key hit the lock on the front door right as his panic was beginning to rise and he swears he's never before heard a sweeter sound even if there is a haunting lilt underlying the scrape of key in tumbler to add to his good scare.

She enters knocking the door open with her hip, sunglasses on and grocery bags in her hands. She curses when her keys drop out of her hands and to the floor. Wicked sunlight streams in after her and rushes up to torment him for a quick short moment before she slams the door with the same hip if reverse side. She moves past him to the kitchen at the back of the place and quickly out of sight. He shifts on the couch momentarily contemplating getting up when the Mistress returns carrying a tray and he thinks better of it when she begins her medical ministrations on him once again.

"You act like it's the first time you've been shot Jackie, you big pussy," she scolds Jackie boy when he winces when she begins to change the dressings.

He shoots her a 'fuck you' glance which is mostly punchless as he lacks the force to put anything menacing behind it. The Mistress knows his terrible secret after all. She knows Jackie Boy's mostly bark despite all of the battles and the subsequent battle scars he's managed to amass over the years.

She places a bowl of gumbo near his elbow and throws the TV remote at him as she stands to move over the room giving Jackie another lovely viewing of her ass and hips swaying beneath the black of her dress. She opens a small cabinet to reveal a TV set which Jackie Boy had no idea she even owned. She turns from the open cabinet and Jackie's expression clearly shows how incredulous he feels at the discovery or something equally stupid on his face.

She gives him a scolding look quite similar to his own earlier attempt against her, though unlike his, hers actually has the effect of, well not exactly shaming him, but certainly cowing him for the moment. She grabs a bag from a nearby chair and places the sunglasses back over her eyes so now Jackie really has no idea what she's thinking.

"Where're you going," he asks her too plain dumb to decipher what she's up to while leaving her baffled for a moment though he cannot really tell past the big sunglasses shielding more than her eyes for the moment.

"I'm going to work you asshole. Just like a regular goddamn person, gotta open up my shop because its ten and I'm late as it is," Jackie's jaw is agape to clearly show his inability to comprehend this simple statement as she continues.

"Yeah it's something normal people do," she says, "don't worry you'll be fine and I'll be back after dark." He doesn't immediately reply and she waits a moment for something and then shrugs her shoulders. A breath escapes from her sounding an awful lot like an elongated uggghh or something of equal value before she heads out the door and leaves him to his own devices alone in her home much to his surprise.

She returns as promised well after dark with some red beans and rice because it is Monday in New Orleans after all, Jackie's hopefully for some smoked sausage with it and fresh French bread realizing he must have been hungrier than he though as he ate fast and was implored to slow down and taste it.

"You back with us there Jackie Boy," she asks him as she hovers nearby to tend to him should he need it. He waves her away as he slowly rises up to a seated positon on the couch and nods his head that he is indeed back here with her. She rises anyway heading to her kitchen where she rummages around for short period and then returns with a large mug which she hands to Jackie Boy with the command to drink implicit if unsaid.

"So, how you feeling now Jackie Boy," The Mistress asks the question trying not to tinge it with sarcasm.

"Like hell," Jackie says feeling it as an ironic understatement of some sort or variety.

"I'm not surprised," The Mistress says, "all things considered."

"Thought I'd told you that this hero shit wasn't for you Jackie Boy," she continues, "so why do you insist on getting yourself into these situations. Didn't you tell me that the girl herself told you she didn't need it?"

Her statement is met by his angry silence as The Mistress realizes something else. She stops tending to him to sit back on the couch to contemplate the thought for a moment.

"She told you to give the hero shit up didn't she," The Mistress says more like a statement than a question. Jackie Boy merely mutters something back at her letting her know she's right. She presses the antibacterial sprayed rag deeper into his cut eliciting an audible ouch and a scowl from him. She then stands and walks off from him on the couch but doesn't go far as she turns on her heel and looks at him tapping her hands one on top of the other in front of her as she debates about saying what was on her mind.

"You need to stop this hero shit Jackie," she says as she gets up to get some more hot water for cleaning another round of fresh wounds.

It's a phrase he's heard before, spoken not so long ago by the girl who got away and damn near in the same tone if not a similar circumstantial list of details. Perhaps unsurprisingly, he has found the phraseology used so often lately in combination with his particular talent of late to find himself in exactly these types of situations.

"I'd ask if you weren't smarter than this, but smart never has been your problem now has it Jackie," she says as she returns to sit back on the couch at his knee. She pours the hot water into a bowl with a towel in it to thoroughly soak it. She picks the towel up and wrings the water from it unconcerned with the heat which most certainly must be punishing her hands before she sets to working at putting him back together again one more time. It's a never ending patchwork piecemealed mess but he doesn't deign to reply to her obviously rhetorical statement.

"It's bull stubbornness hurting you," she says as close to hurt as she can get in this instance with him, "that damned hard head of yours Jackie!"

It's the pure exasperation she's feeling vocalized and Jackie has not one bit of blame against her because it would be straight wrong. Jackie knows when The Mistress clearly had a plain and near indisputable right to it, rightly earned.

"Where're you going," she asks a bit startled at the suddenness of his abrupt rise from the couch as he heeds the call which is solidly and alone within his own skull, a call begging for action even if he doesn't know the type required or where to apply it.

"Things to do," he says as he stands up a little wobbly but defiant and offering a daring stare towards The Mistress to try to stop him. The Mistress simply looks disappointed with him somehow as she sits with her legs underneath her on the couch looking at him. She sighs before taking in a much deeper breath which she loudly expels as she watches him, partly admiring his resilience while knowing it was what was going to get him killed permanently this time.

She knows that death's waiting on Jackie, been waiting on him a good long time and won't be denied this time when he steps back out to the street and away from the comparative safety offered within the walls of her home.

Jackie looks about him for something though neither of them can guess at what, he's wearing everything he has or brought with him when he'd first darkened her door step. He turns and stops to really look at her and more importantly really allow her to look at him and through him it feels. He's feeling rather thin tonight like he's not all really here. He tells himself it's because of his encounters with the thin man which had him feeling this way tonight as opposed to The Mistress' ability to see things as they really are.

She knew things others were not given to know and Jackie could damn sure feel it right now as she watched him. He tried hard to convince himself it was a sad look of hers. A defeated look like she already knew what his outcome was to be. Hell, Jackie himself could tell you the most likely outcome of all this running about, it would be unfair though. Just because he was a bull rushing towards the matador and certain death at the point of a sword didn't mean the Mistress herself didn't see it, know it and still wish him some other less specific death than the one she saw in all its details. Jackie, for his part, simply knew it to be his current destination.

He feels like he should say something to her before he leaves though which has caused him to be rooted to this spot currently. Both of them know there's nothing which could be said. She expects no thank you from him, which is a relief as Jackie knows the words would be nothing but insufficient. Just as there were no words she could speak top him to persuade him off of this course.

"You're not going to try to talk me out of it," Jackie says his voice raggedy and coarse. She shoots him a 'are you kidding me,' look before shrugging her shoulders.

"I'm not going to waste my time,' she says rather harshly, "there's no use in trying when you're so damned determined to return yourself to dead."

"I'd thought you'd said I wasn't dead," Jackie Boy finally manages to say after a long moment's pause to digest the conversation. The Mistress looks away from him to hide her anger with him, at his insistence at picking this fight with her as well as his continued insistence to go out and play hero when it wasn't going to anybody any good. It couldn't bring back the dead or change what's happened. She's mad at the thin man for perpetuating Jackie Boy's hero streak thinking to have a word with the man the next time she saw him.

"No," she says finally exasperated with him, "I said that how you weren't dead wasn't from a lack of trying."

Her reply only makes his head pound more with the return of the damn headache to alter his perception of realty. He's a bit surprised that she has missed the obvious and he feels the need to remind her that he is already dead. She rolls her eyes and turns her head away from him with a loud scoff and refuses to return her gave to him.

"So there's that," Jackie says just to break the silence.

"Yeah," she says her tone sounding sorrowful, "So there's that," but now she's no longer looking at him. Instead, she's looking off to the back of the house or some future he doesn't want to know and won't ask her.

There's another long silence as if both are waiting on the other to say something, anything but there's nothing to be added and neither are given to sentiment either. This is the longest goodbye between them ever in a twist of ironic because both know he's going to go and both know there's nothing more to say about it or anything else. They both wait while he shifts where he stands and she sinks deeper into the couch still not looking at him.

"I'm going," he says as he half steps towards the door waiting for what he doesn't know. For a word perhaps, any word at all from her which comes at the last possible moment it can, right before he steps out across her stoop down two steps and out into the street.

"Just go already Jackie," she says in clear resignation. "Just know that this is goodbye Jackie, goodbye forever," she says and it chases after him settling on his shoulders and haunting him as he moves away from her house and deeper into the Quarter.

Vengeance

The Mistress had once and not so long ago, told Jackie Boy how the gods must find him amusing to simultaneously keep him alive to continue his streak of stumbling along on his streak of bad luck. Jackie hadn't been pleased with the theory posited by The Mistress at the time finding it unpleasant to think that the only reason he was still here was because the gods found him amusing and had left him to see what havoc he could make. To see what chaos he could sow as he went stumbling about simply because the gods needed original content for viewing as well and what better way to spin a story than the serialization of Jackie Boy's pain.

It was a theory which had been lent credence recently with all that had happened to him and feeling like a sentence passed for his crime for reaching for things he's not supposed to have had. Jackie remembers the girl and sorrow comes up to choke him a horrible gagging sound as he tries to tamp it back down with extreme prejudicial force. It had been a nice little dream, if a brief one, until Jackie remembers that nightmares are dreams too. Dreams are like ghosts though. All ethereal and transient by their nature like these current fever dreams of his. But it's the only place he can still find her, can still enjoy her ghostly charms knowing it's a dream so he can tell himself anything to overcome the ache of missing her.

This remembrance of the girl would hold except that Jackie Boy knows that she's dead and gone now and he feels he's pretty damned sure how he's the cause. He's the reason for one dead girl lying broken in the pavers because he'd dared to reach to think for a moment he'd earned anything of that nature. The girl dead and gone and Jackie was neither and an easy trade to make were there any to oversee the details of the transaction. But it was not to be. Not for the likes of him clearly with the decision already made and the girl dead and gone and Ol' Jackie Boy not so much.

Jackie Boy left here in continued existence with plenty of time to ponder the fates and their choices in leaving him here and taking her. And then Jackie Boy remembers that the thin man, the Voodoo Man, had promised him vengeance and he knew how vengeance was the most noble purpose on the planet and one which, if not blessed, was at least condoned by the gods and he sets his sights on achieving it.

He has to let Sissy go first though. It's only fair to let her go now when he had proven himself unable to hold on to her in the here and now physical world. Letting her go is both an altruistic act and a selfish one. It's a selfish act for how it frees Jackie boy to go out and seek the vengeance the thin man had promised him. No matter how one parsed it, vengeance was never for the departed. It was always for the living.

The Road to Hell

Jackie Boy's sitting in a bar in the lower Quarter with a pint in hand deciding on the course he should best steer to achieve the vengeance he seeks. He's thinking about earlier he'd decided how somebody must know something and it had taken him to the club and Terry and the same conclusion still holds here as decides to start again with Terry at the *gentlemen's* club. Terry was the man to tell him who the man with the gun was and who it was that the gun man worked for and if not, than Bobby D most certainly would. It wasn't much to go on, but it was at least a path to start his trek down.

Jackie Boy returns to the club to look for Terry and finds find him in his office with two girls from the club seeing to his needs. Jackie Boy grabs a stapler from off the desk and wings it at Terry who looks about with a 'what the fuck' expression on his face until he sees Jackie Boy in the other side of the desk and his anger rises to a very dark shade of red. The dark shade of red heads towards purple when Jackie Boy dismisses the girls with a mention of a business conversation he has to have with Terry.

The girls scamper out and Jackie Boy turns his full attention to Terry who doesn't bother to bluster with threats of any kind this time. He scrambles for what Jackie Boy assumes is his pants and belt but Terry's reaching for his desk drawer and the gun he put in there since the shit with Jackie Boy had gone down. Jackie Boy recognizes the pistil when the drawer is fully opened and acting on instinct he moves around the desk and punches Terry in the face.

It doesn't quite have the effect Jackie Boy had hoped for as Terry has managed to still grab the gun and has brought it up towards Jackie Boy. Jackie punches Terry's wounded hand which produces a yelp from him and a shot from the pistol to zing past Jackie Boy's ear. Jackie Boy's so pissed off about this that he rips the pistol out of Terry's hands and shoots him multiple times with it to leave a bloody mess in the chair.

'Fuck,' Jackie Boy thinks nearly out loud when the smoke clears, so much for asking Terry anything. He pockets the gun and quickly exits the premises thinking strangely about the road to hell and how this was the kind of step which put a person on it. Of course, Jackie's been told so many times he was going to hell that it meant little to nothing anymore. He thought how people kept throwing damnation around so casually as if they were so certain of their own redemption with the stacking of all of their chips on one god and his benevolence.

Jackie Boy had seen too much over his life though to give much countenance to the whole benevolent thing. He knew far better than most that the things you do in life you carry with you and aint no need of punishment or divine judgment. The things done are waking punishment every damnded day which is why he generally woke to curse the start of every new one he had to face. Good intentions or not, outcomes mattered more. Outcomes marked against ones general ledger or down in the big book or whatever the hell was being used to keep tabs on these kinds of things by whatever powers there are and all so much nonsense.

Still, Jackie Boy should have heeded the advice which had been tossed about for so long it damn near qualified as ancient lore. It was about minding one's own business and not getting involved in other people's shit. Straight good advice and he really ought to get it tattooed on some place on his body like on his forehead so he could be reminded of knowing better every damn day.

The road to hell it turns out, isn't paved with gold, nor is it an especially difficult drive. It's a mostly and remarkably smooth sailing kind of ride best intentions or otherwise. Jackie doesn't believe in hell though, and if there's no hell, then that's one less thing to worry about.

Joey Bones, Cleaner

Joey Bones and King had been discussing the character known as Ol' Jackie Boy who, through sheer persistence or pig-headed stubbornness, has made a nuisance of himself in their operations in the city. It had started out with a simple altercation in the club which Bobby D ran for them through his boy Terry which was bad enough as they didn't like any interference with the running of their day-to-day business. This was a problem they could handle and discretely too, however displeased they were that it had happened.

The problem they'd had was how it hadn't stopped there and the continued desire of this Jackie Boy to play hero which was troublesome. Heroes made noise after all, noise which couldn't be ignored. This hero Jackie Boy had until he'd gotten himself shot down dead. It was the only solution which worked to dissuade him away from his notion of playing hero.

They'd been left with little choice with the hero after their idea to hurt the hero Jackie Boy through the girl. It had only led to more interference from the hero until Joey Bones himself had to attend to the hero personally. Now that the hero had been cleared from the decks it was time to clean up some of the residuals which the hero had uncovered as liabilities within King's organization much to his displeasure.

"There's a few things that have to be attended to Joey," King says as he rises from his desk damn near clapping his hands and smiling totally unnerving Joey for a moment despite knowing the conclusion King has reached. Joey Bones knows King means for him to take care of Terry because the man's incompetence could no longer be tolerated and removing him went without saying.

King and Joey Bones still had some residual mess to clean up and up near the top of their list was to take care of Terry. It was Terry after all who was supposed to be managing their club where all the trouble with the hero had started. Terry has proven his incompetence with his inability to deal with or contain the hero allowing him to become a problem blown out of all proportion.

Joey Bones decides that when he's done with Terry how he'll put in a call to King's pet cops to report the killing in an effort to put the kill on the hero Jackie Boy. The hero had already done part of the work for them with the very public and loud dispute he'd had with Terry not once but twice now.

Joey Bones doesn't have to look hard for Terry as the man didn't exactly keep his whereabouts unknown and spent most of his time at the club. Joey Bones goes there first heading upstairs where he finds Terry shot dead behind his desk. Joey questions the staff and then the girls who were there and they all describe a character who sounds very much like the dead hero.

Joey Bones doesn't want to believe it. He finds it hard to accept except for the fact of how this stupid mother fucker who should be dead wasn't with enough witnesses to make him believe it. What seals it is the security footage he looks at which shows him the hero. Dammit all to hell Joey Bones thinks as he picks up the phone to make a call for the Tweedles to help cover up this mess made by the hero.

He doesn't wait for them to arrive as he heads off to King to tell him all he's seen while cursing himself for not heading off the hero from the first moment he'd reared his head. A mistake which Joey bones was sure to correct in short order.

King's Resolve

Joey Bones returns to King's place and tells King about the return of the hero to the club. King looks at Joey Bones with a large displeased look saying to Joey how King thought Joey had shot him. Joey looks back at King and says the only thing he can which is how he'd thought so to. Joey goes on to state how he cannot explain it other than how the fucker must be blessed or something which earns Joey Bones a 'you've got to be shitting me,' look from King.

King's displeasure grows when Joey Bones tells him how if the hero kept to his course, he'd end up coming straight for them sooner or later. He asks Joey where the hero is now and Joey tells him he doesn't know.

King thinks about this for a moment and then decides that someone knows how to get a hold of this hero and that this same someone was Bobby D. Bobby D was, after all, the one who was responsible for both Terry and the hero Jackie Boy. Bobby D was the link to the two men and to the *gentlemen's* club which has been the epicenter from which all of his current troubles had radiated out from.

Gentlemen's club was what Bobby D preferred to call the place like he's got pretentions and hates it when other people call it a strip club. King smiles at the statement, a wide smile cause know he knows exactly where to start now. He knows that Bobby D's long past an overdue visit. King rises up grabs his coat and heads for the door grabbing Joey and pulling him into his orbit as he heads for the door.

"Where we going boss," Joey asks and King replies through his wide smile, "Bobby D's my man, Bobby D's."

King had never really liked how Bobby D had put Terry into the job which seemed too large for him. King had let it pass even though he'd thought from the start how he was going to have to do something about Terry one day and had been waiting for the moment ever since. Terry had, at first, surprised him by keeping the trouble down and the money rolling in at the club which in turn had King and Bones willing to overlook how Terry took certain liberties with the girls.

He just hadn't expected Terry to be exposed this soon and he had this Jackie Boy character to thank for having brought the day of dealing with Terry into the present, much to King's displeasure. It's fit punishment. King surmises. for allowing it in the first place which made it his fault he knew. King won't let on, but he's deeply disturbed by this Jackie Boy's ability to continually disrupt his business dealings seemingly at will. This dumb bastard Jackie Boy simply stumbling along dumb and mammoth beast like smashing things in his path without awareness of the carnage spewn in his wake.

They head further Uptown from their location to where Bobby D is known to reside. Bobby D's very surprised to see King at his door. Bobby D's leery too of the reasons for what can only be considered an official state visit. King clearly not there to negotiate. Bobby had heard about some incident down at the club but it hadn't seemed out of the ordinary at the time and certainly not enough to warrant a visit from 'The Man' King himself.

"Bobby D, as I live and breathe," King says as he sits down in a chair Joey has picked out for him. King sits down and doesn't say any more which makes Bobby D very nervous with their combined presence. He's taking care to be very cautious and mindful of the courtesies. He didn't want to provoke King in any way here even though he suspects and correctly too mind you, that this is not going to go well for him

Bobby D wondered, and not for the first time either, exactly what Jackie Boy had gotten them into and how deep. Unfortunately, he was about to find out as Joey Bones enters into Bobby D's space without invitation to stand menacingly near him. Joey placing himself easily within arm's reach, just a quick snap punch away from Bobby D. Bobby D has known Joey Bones back when he was still a fighter and from around the ring a couple of times over the years. He'd even seen Joey fight and knew how quick Joey could be when he was of a mind to which had Bobby D deciding to do his best to ensure that didn't come to pass, to give no reason for Joey Bones to display his prowess.

Bobby D wasn't a straight up criminal then or now like Joey Bones had become, and sure as shit wasn't anywhere near King's level either. He sat tight on the borderline between the two sides of the law which tended to make him useful in their activities. It had always been a profitable relationship for all involved while Bobby D worked both sides of the line.

King starts with hello and some small talk intermixing it with some questions asked of Bobby D. They're not straight ahead questions though, they're dancing all around type questions when Bobby D's pretty sure all King and Joey Bones want is Jackie Boy and where he might be. It left Bobby D wondering why he didn't just get to it and stop all this oblique shit.

Bobby D soon gets his answer when Joey Bones smashes his hand against the desk with his own iron like fist. Bobby D swears he can hear his bones crunching proving the truth of Joey's nickname and begins to become really frightened about where this was going.

"Damn Bobby, why are you making my man work so hard now," King asks in a calm manner sitting in the chair and making it a throne beaming down his countenance from on high like he really would rather not be doing this.

"So, where is this Jackie Boy of yours," King finally asks him but Bobby D doesn't immediately answer him as he's holding his smashed hand wincing from the pain. It's not out of any great loyalty to Jackie or anything or even to protect his sister's putz of a kid Terry. Mostly Bobby D doesn't answer out of a strange fear at guessing wrong on the answer which King and Joey Bones desire.

"I don't know man," Bobby D says still hurting from the smashing of his hand and knowing it was the wrong thing to say the minute it escapes his mouth.

"Unbelievable," King says shaking his head before passing a signal to Joey Bones who picks Bobby D up while simultaneously playing a rhythm on his kidneys before allowing him to fall back to the floor in a lump.

King leans over and looks at Bobby a moment disgusted though Bobby D isn't clear on the what or why of it and in too much pain to care other than to note how King himself was the catalyst for this particular result. Bobby D lies there on the floor trying hard to remember how to breathe and questioning his foolishness at trying to work anything in Jackie Boy's favor. This seems to be his just reward for that particular piece of work and so much for good deeds done. From the files of 'he shoulda known better.'

Sure, Bobby D had known Jackie Boy a long, long time. Straight out of once upon a time if one cared to go back that far. So far back that Bobby D sure as shit should have known better, right as he sure as shit he should have stayed the far as fuck away from it as he could. Bobby D being more qualified than any to know Jackie's propensity, nice word there, for sinking his ass into the deepest part of the worst kind of trouble which could be found and had brought Joey Bones and King to his door.

He must have been getting soft or sentimental or some such shit to override his self-preservation or good sense or something to have done Ol' Jackie any favors. He should've employed the ten foot pole theory you hear so much about but it was too late for any of it. Hell it was way past, way too late for that.

Joey Bones leans into Bobby D who knows he's never going to leave this shitty little room of his alive. The realization strangely empowers Bobby D to defiance in the old nothing to lose rubric. He didn't have any answers to give King anyway as he honestly didn't know where Jackie Boy was and tells King this. King pauses as he thinks on the newly acquired information.

"You must know how to find him though," King surmises aloud. "You found him once for this job at the strip club after all.

King lets it hang there tempting Bobby D to correct him on this description and tell him to call it a *gentlemen's* club like such a thing could matter here in this instance.

"I don't know shit man," Bobby D responds to King who calmly reaches for his revolver. He frees the cylinder and removes four out of five bullets putting them into his pocket while talking to Bobby D.

"You a gambling man there Bobby," asks King as he spins the cylinder and prepares for a game of Russian Roulette.

"I don't know anything," Bobby D screams now.

"You know something," King says pointing the pistol in Bobby D's general direction.

"I don't, I don't," Bobby D pleads now which King finds so pathetic.

"If you don't then what good are you," King says standing to walk a step or two away from Bobby D. Enough space ceded for Bobby D to think there might be a reprieve in his immediate future. There isn't as Joey Bones walks over besides King who hands the big revolver over to him. Joey's tsk tsking as he moves to stand over Bobby D and looks down at him.

"Make your peace then mother fucker," Joey says to him as the pistol flashes out. Bobby D crosses his arms over his eyes so he doesn't have to see it coming when Joey puts a bullet into his head. Joey Bones leans over the newly made corpse before smashing the teeth in with the butt of the pistol's handgrip. He stands up straight to follow King who stands a step or two ahead of him looking at him quizzically. Joey simply shrugs his shoulders in a 'what' kind of way.

"What was that for," King asks him thinking it was strictly unnecessary and Joey looks at him obtuse and oblivious

"That," Joey asks with King pointing back at the remains of Bobby D. Joey looks back for a moment and King swears he can hear the wheels turning, grinding perhaps, for the reason behind smashing in Bobby D's teeth.

"Oh, that," Joey says and another shrug of his shoulders is offered. "Never did like the motherfucker anyway." King simply nods his head in agreement like this makes perfect sense.

Uptown Saturday Night

Jackie Boy heads uptown to Bobby D's place and lets himself in when he gets there. He climbs up the stairs to find Bobby D sprawled out on the floor behind the desk in his office. Nothing else is much out of place as far as Jackie can tell as he looks about the place. He squats down to take a closer look at Bobby D which he'd been avoiding doing since he walked in.

He didn't want to see Bobby D like this as he was the last tie to any part of Jackie Boy's past and the only person who could even remotely have been described as being closest to Jackie Boy over all the years they'd shared the same miles together.

The poor bastard Bobby D's lying there with his teeth smashed in as a punctuation to the bullet which had been put through his skull. Jackie lowers his head in a moment strictly for honoring the dead. He sighs as he reaches out to grab and squeeze one of Bobby D's hands.

The poor bastard deserved better Jackie thought, a better fate than this after all of the things they'd both seen and been through. Ignominious endings but, perhaps also inevitable, when you're in the line of work with the kind of people it drew to it which Bobby D had been in. Mind you, Jackie Boy didn't exclude himself from the list as he leaves another person who was unable to escape the wrath meant for him.

Jackie Boy stands up and moves to Bobby D's desk. He reaches into an open drawer and pulls out a bottle of Beam which he knew that Bobby D always kept there. Damn thing was nearly full too to boot. Jackie unscrews the cap and takes a good long hard slug. He looks over at the body of his friend and pulls another slug from the bottle before standing up. He pours out the balance of the bottle's contents to soak into the carpet around Bobby D and then puts the bottle back in the desk.

Jackie heads for the door knowing full well where he's going next and what's waiting for him there. There'd only ever been the one answer about where to go to settle things even if Jackie Boy had spent most of his time trying to ignore it. It was time for our intrepid hero Ol' Jackie Boy to pay a visit to the only man who could orchestrate all of this against him. The man Jackie Boy was going to see now was a man with the pretentiousness to call himself King.

The Man Called King

Joey Bones knows that with the murder of Bobby D on top of the girl's death that he'd left the hero Jackie Boy nowhere else to turn but to come straight at them. It was a lazy strategy, if effective, as nothing else had dissuaded the hero from his mission and this strategy at least had the advantage of bringing him to them instead of trying to finish him.

Joey Bones is briefly rethinking the strategy through. A brief pause to entertain the idea of careful what you wish for, you just might get it. His experience as a fighter told Joey Bones that advantages gained could vanish in an instant and turn to detrimental. King had called for the hero's destruction and wrought plenty around the man so he was now a cliché himself. Jackie Boy had now become the man with nothing left to loose. And, at least according to the movies, this gave him a certain amount of mysterious power and indestructibility until the hero had seen his vengeance through as only then would the hero be allowed to die.

Joey Bones was a better thinker with more knowledge available to him than was readily assumed by most everyone. Joey Bones was a lot of things but dumb, despite appearances to the contrary. It was the way he preferred it, using it as a ruse a feint to throw people off as he liked it when he was underestimated. A better thinker than even King gave him credit for unable to see past his blank expression and smashed boxer's nose.

Joey Bones and King have lined up some of their soldiers arming them with the intention of ending this hero's storyline. Joey Bones was curious to see if they'd be able to do the job and how many would fall in the attempt. The predetermined course of the fight is the hero himself will fall.

It's how Joey knows King is thinking of the situation coming. King's not concerning himself with the hero and whatever he's prepared to do when he arrives though his goals are the same as theirs. The man intends to deal out death and in turn seems willing to accept his own as the cost. Death is a certainty in the coming evening, though whose is unclear. Joey Bones is alright with the thought. He's known for quite some time now that death was always coming and very little could be done about it

Joey Bones is frankly surprised it has taken the hero this long to come starlight for them. From what Joey had learned of the hero so far, the man seemed to have only the one course of straight ahead to steer. They and the hero have been within proximity of one another all throughout this story and it shouldn't have taken this long to bring it to a resolution Joey thinks to himself. He's thinking too much about it he knows. All that matters is that the hero's coming tonight bringing the showdown they'd all been circling round for a few days now. He smiles with the thought of it, glad for a resolution one way or the other. He grabs and pockets a second pistol for the occasion and waits for the hero to show.

King's sits at his desk with a drink in his hand. He looks over and reaches into the top side drawer of his desk where he keeps his pistol, clips and ammo. He pulls them out and checks that the pistol is loaded even though he knows it's loaded and in good working order which it was

The gun was always in this condition as King had always though it would be flat straight stupid to have a pistol and have it anything less than full operational capacity and strength. What's the use of strength of arms if you don't care for them so they can care for you when the time arises after all.

King sets the pistol on the desk in front of him briefly wishing for a moment he was more heavily armed. He's trying not to show it, but he's feeling apprehensive about the news Joey Bones has relayed to him of the hero's intent to come to them. This damn hero, who refused to die, refused to keep himself out of their activities.

King sits looking at the pistol which for years he'd often thought of as his right hand man. He recalls how he'd made his name and his place in the world with this same pistol or others like it. How he'd risen to the position and the self-chosen moniker of King and demanding to be addressed as such accorded the respect of the title. He'd done exactly like Walken had in that movie he'd based his rise on though first held made his reputation, at least partly, with the pistol. It was how King had defined himself then before he'd been able to redefine himself.

This Jackie Boy situation called for a return to King's old ways he thought as he placed the pistol on the desk in front of him. King was returning back to the right hand man who'd always stood by him and done right by him for longer than any one person or thing including Joey Bones.

King looks at Joey Bones to see if he's feeling any nervousness, but Joey Bones was standing there all stoic and stone faced. If King was worried, he dared not showing it as he knows how it would be taken for weakness if he should. He does notice how Joey Bones is himself strapped with a second pistol and decides this is not a bad idea at all. He opens the second bottom drawer of his desk and extracts a second pistol. He checks this one as he did the first repeating the thoughts and actions like it's a religious mantra despite the fact he's not feeling religious. He's simply a professional taking up the tools of his trade. The pistols the tools of his profession, a profession he's traded, if not in recent memory. He's not certain whether to curse this would be hero or to thank him for the opportunity he presents here today.

King places the second pistol on the desk in front of him next to the first. He reaches for the phone to make a quick call for a girl so he can get blown, maybe even a quickie to chase the stress away because he wants to be loose when all the shit starts after all.

Men with Guns

Jackie Boy remembered King from before he'd been called by the name King, if only by his own insistence from his time with the NOPD. The man calling himself King was a self-styled gangster who had risen to control a good portion of the city's crime and known for his ruthlessness. He was the man who owned the club where this had all started and been behind the gun man in the square as well.

King was the man to see to settle this little dispute once and for all which Jackie Boy had always known but had also purposefully tried to avoid. He hadn't wanted to escalate the whole affair way out of proportion though it was certainly well past at this point. He'd already passed the point of being knee deep in the shit about a day or so ago and now knee deep was no longer the right description for where he was presently.

Jackie moves through the streets of the city making his way to the place of the man called King. He tries the door and finds it's unlocked which tells him he's expected. Good, he thinks, less work before they can all get straight to it. He walks through the place heading down a hallway to where he sees a light on. He steps into a room filled with guys and guns and one smoking hot woman in a short black dress to the left of the man at the desk. The set is completed with the arrival of one dumb mother fucker, our hero, standing at the front of it all.

Jackie assumes that the man behind the desk is King. This man King is impeccably dressed in a crème colored suit well-tailored for broad shoulders and the ubiquitous pistol shoulder rig beneath his coat. He wears a dark merlot colored shirt with an even darker merlot colored tie to compliment the coat. King's most striking aspect in every sense of the word are his intense eyes which pierce right through you when he deigns to look right at you like he's doing right now to our intrepid hero Jackie Boy.

Jackie Boy though is luckily too obtuse, too stubborn or straight plain too fucking tired for the death stare to have much effect on him now. Jackie sees the man has two pistols lying on the desk in front of him telling him how he'd clearly been expected.

Jackie Boy keeps his eyes on the man to King's right who looks an awful lot like the gunman he'd met in an alley a short while back deciding he would try to shoot him first if given the option. Jackie's pistol is in his hand hanging at his side as he takes the scene in. He decides to begin without pleasantries or introductions, feeling that they're mostly unnecessary here as all parties know the why of the gathering. He raises his pistol straight at the man behind the desk. King looks at the man who would be a hero and laughs at him.

"So you're the hero," King says to him as Jackie Boy stands before him, "Come to die have you?"

Jackie Boy just shrugs at King before he tells King that he needn't have killed the girl when she'd done nothing to him after all which King merely shrugs off.

"All this over some girl," King says incredulously, "Hope she was worth it."

"I loved that little girl," Jackie says like it explains it all.

Laughs from around the room follow the declaration and afterwards incredulity dominates the room as the enemy parties look from one to the other at an explanation which seems beyond preposterous. It's too blatantly dull an explanation to contemplate or understand especially in light of all the damage wrought over the past few days. All of the disruptions and upheavals caused by this stupid mother fucker who thought he was in love with a girl.

"Are you fucking kidding me," King demands, "please tell me you're kidding me."

King's face falls when he sees the seriousness look written on Jackie Boy's face. He realizes that this dumb bastard was serious about it and seemingly hell bent on doubling down on it.

"Love," King says, "right, sure. What do you make of that?"

This last part is directed to Joey Bones over on his right who snorts back a laugh before he repeats King's assessment of, 'love, right, sure,' adding in his two cents and finishing with, 'sure what the hell.'

Jackie Boy's a bit perplexed by their cavalier attitude. He pauses to consider his actions which have brought everyone to this point. Jackie does a quick reevaluation to possibly arrive at a different conclusion than this one without seeing any other one which he'd rather be at.

"It doesn't change any damn thing," Jackie finally says after letting what feels like long moments pass by as the tension continued ratcheting up to fill the room.

"I'm here, you're here," and then his voice trails off with him looking down at his gun to finish his implication voiced.

"Going to see it through then are you," the man called King asks aloud.

"You took the last thing from me I had to lose, so," and he lets it hang there.

"You still have one more there to give hero, your life" King says. "You can't possible think you'll get out of here alive after all."

Jackie nods his head in agreement while looking down at his pistol, it's something he'd understood, had known from before he'd walked into the place.

"Yeah," he says, "I'm all good with that."

Jackie Boy nods his head again before he raises the pistol. He pulls the trigger and shots are fired.

A Secondary Author's Note

The believed origination of the phrase "the road to hell is paved with good intentions," is thought to have originated with Saint Bernard of Clairvaux who wrote, "*L'enfer est plein de bonnes volontés et désirs.*" (Hell is full of good wishes and desires).

ABOUT THE AUTHOR

Jack Kelly is a pseudonym.

He previously wrote three other stories also
set in the City Of New Orleans.
The three stories feature a very different
protagonist from this one.
To read about the Haunt that Rocks The
Crescent, please read:

WAKE THE DEAD
RISE A HAUNT
THE TERRIBLE FRIGHT

All books are available at Amazon.com and Kindle